MW00577022

STYRBIORN
THE
STRONG

STYRBIORN

THE

·STRONG·

E. R. Eddison

Afterword by Paul Edmund Thomas

Illustrations by Keith Henderson

University of Minnesota Press
Minneapolis
London

To my brother Colin
I dedicate this book

First published in the United States by Albert & Charles Boni, 1926

First University of Minnesota Press edition, 2011

Copyright 2011 by Anne Hesketh Al-Shahi.
Original copyright 1926 by E. R. Eddison; renewed 1953
by Winifred Grace Eddison and Jean Gudrun Rucker Latham.

Afterword copyright 2011 by Paul Edmund Thomas

All rights reserved. No part of this publication may be reproduced, stored in
a retrieval system, or transmitted, in any form or by any means, electronic,
mechanical, photocopying, recording, or otherwise, without the prior written
permission of the publisher.

Published by the University of Minnesota Press
111 Third Avenue South, Suite 290
Minneapolis, MN 55401-2520
http://www.upress.umn.edu

Library of Congress Cataloging-in-Publication Data

Eddison, Eric Rücker, 1882–1945.
Styrbiorn the strong / E. R. Eddison ; afterword by Paul Edmund Thomas ;
illustrations by Keith Henderson. — 1st University of Minnesota Press ed.
p. cm.
ISBN 978-0-8166-7755-9 (pb : alk. paper)
1. Styrbjörn Starki, d. 983—Fiction. I. Title.
PR6009.D3S79 2011
823'.912—dc23
2011037296

Printed in the United States of America on acid-free paper

The University of Minnesota is an equal-opportunity educator and employer.

17 16 15 14 13 12 11   10 9 8 7 6 5 4 3 2 1

·CONTENTS·

E. R. Eddison's Unpublished
Letter of Introduction
to *Styrbiorn the Strong*

[Archived in the Public Library of Leeds, this Letter of Introduction is undated but was written in July or August 1922. There is no extant record either of Eddison's providing this piece for Jonathan Cape's consideration or of Cape's reasons for omitting it from the book as published in 1926, so it is possible Eddison never showed it to Cape. —P. E. Thomas]

Dear Colin:

There is no saga of the Swedish prince after whom this story is named. If there were, I do not think my story would have been written. For it is not my study to emulate a writer for whose other work I have a respect, in treating the sagas as Tate & Cibber treated Shakespeare, tricking out these imperishable prose epics of the north with modern fripperies of sentimental love interest and psychological disquisition: or (if he prefers it so) rewriting these fusty old chronicles into marketable novels of today. I am so simple as to believe that those grand stories are so elemental, so beautiful, so firm set in the soil of life, that they are quite able to look after themselves. All we want (and we may have to wait for it) is a translator of the rank of Dasent or Morris to carry on the work they so splendidly began.

7

My story, then, is neither an imitation, nor yet an "improved" edition, of a saga. The spirit of the sagas I hope is in it, for that is a living spirit: one of the greatest, as I think, that human history can show. But I have not sought to ape the sagas' bodily build and gait, but have told my story in my own way, the best I could.

The accepted date of the battle of Fyrisfield is the year 983, and my chief authority is the short *Þáttr Styrbjarnar Sviakappa*, printed in the *Lives of the Kings* (Fornmannasögur, Vol. V, pp. 245–51: Copenhagen, 1830). This in brief gives the bald facts: Styrbiorn at his father's howe; Aki's slaying; the trouble with the bonders; the viking expedition; his captainship of the Jomsburgers; press-gang treatment of King Harald Gormson; marriage to Queen Thyri; the three days' fight at Fyrisfield, with Thorgnyr's tactics and the rival invocations to Odin and to Thor.

Styrbiorn's name has sounded in my memory like a drum ever since, twenty years ago, I first read the passing reference to him in the *Eyrbyggja Saga*:

> When Biorn came out over the sea, he went
> south to Denmark, and then south further to
> Jomsburg, and in those days was Palnatoki
> captain of the Jomsburg vikings. Biorn entered
> into covenant with them, and was called a
> champion there. He was in Jomsburg when
> Styrbiorn the Strong won it and he went to
> Sweden when they of Jomsburg gave aid to
> Styrbiorn, and was withal at the battle at

Fyrisfield where Styrbiorn fell, and fled thence
to the woods with the other Jomsburg vikings.

And again, in the *Heimskringla*, the speech of Olaf the
Swede-King to Hialti Skeggison:

Then Harald Gormson laid Norway to his
own realm and revenue, and yet we deemed
King Harald Gormson as of lesser might than
the Upsala kings, inasmuch as Styrbiorn, our
kinsman, cowed him, so that Harald became his
man; but Eric the Victorious, my father, strode
over the head of Styrbiorn when they tried it
out between them.

Those two quotations are the father and the mother of
this book.

For the share of Sigrid the Haughty in the drama there
is no authority, but it is not I think out of keeping with the
character of that imperious and fatal Queen. Her marriage
to and subsequent separation from Eric, and the homage
paid in his father's life-time to her son Olaf, are matters of
history. For the personal characters of the two great pro-
tagonists, Eric and Styrbiorn, I am again almost entirely
responsible. Here, and elsewhere in my story where I have
portrayed the persons and characters of real people, I have
framed my mind not as one who would snatch some cheap
applause by staging puppets in old tremendous scenes and
clothing them with the lordly insignia and mantles of the
dead, which are not lordly only, but piteous too and sacred, as all graves are piteous and sacred. Rather have I,

9

as soberly and reverently as I might, yet with my thoughts bent on life and its humours and splendours, not on the chilling yet hollow menace of annihilation, so set down my story of these great men dead that, if it be granted to me to sit with them at the last at Odin's board, I shall be able without fear and unashamed to shake them by the hand, and find perhaps that they had known even now (as I like to suppose they know) all that I, born in a later, wealthier, better informed, but not a wiser nor a nobler age, thought and guessed and wrote about them.

So here is my book. And because you, being a smaller boy than me, suffered so gallantly many years ago my first saga-madness, to you I dedicate this book.

E. R. Eddison

·AUTHOR'S NOTE·

W̶HEN Biorn came out over the sea, he went south to Denmark, and then south further to Jomsburg, and in those days was Palnatoki captain of the Jomsburg vikings. Biorn entered into covenant with them, and was called a champion there. He was in Jomsburg when Styrbiorn the Strong won it and he went to Sweden when they of Jomsburg gave aid to Styrbiorn, and was withal at the battle at Fyrisfield where Styrbiorn fell, and fled thence to the woods with the other Jomsburg vikings. (*Eyrbyggja Saga*, transl. William Morris and Eirikr Magnússon: Ch. XXIX.)

Then Harald Gormson laid Norway to his own realm and revenue, and yet we deemed King Harald Gormson as of lesser might than the Upsala kings, inasmuch as Styrbiorn, our kinsman, cowed him, so that Harald became his man; but Eric the Victorious, my father, strode over the head of Styrbiorn when they tried it out between them. (*Heimskringla*, same transl.: Vol. 2, Ch. LXXI: speech of Olaf the Swede-King to Hialti Skeggison.)

In the old Northern tongue *ei* is pronounced as in the English *rein: v* like the English *w:* and *j* like the English *y: g* is always hard. The final *i* in proper names (e.g. Helgi) is short. Moldi is pronounced *mouldy:* Jomsburg, *Yŏmsburg*. The *y* in Fyrisfield and in Thyri is short as in *syrup*.

Sidmouth, 2d January, 1926.   E. R. E.

I

On King Olaf's Howe

ERIC the Victorious was in that time King in Upsala, the son of Biorn the Old, the son of Eric, the son of Emund, and had dominion over the Up-Swedes and over the folk of Nether-realm and Southmanland and East and West Gautland and over all countries and kingdoms eastaway from the Elf to the main sea. King Eric was as now in his old years, and was held for a man of mickle might and worship, sitting in that state and stead whereas his forefathers aforetime sat from the days of Ragnar Hairy-breeks; and in their veins was the blood of the kin of the Ynglings, even from that far time when the Gods came first from Asgarth of ancient days, and Yngvi-Frey dwelt among mankind in kingdom in Upsala.

Now when King Biorn the Old was come to die, he left his two sons Eric and Olaf joint Kings in Sweden, and forty years they reigned together in good brotherly love and friendship. King Olaf Biornson had to wife Ingibiorg, daughter of Earl Thrand of Sula. Their children were Thora and Thurid and Asdis and Aud. Ungainly it seemed to King Olaf that he should get none but girl-children. Howso, in the end it befell that Queen Ingibiorg was brought to bed of a man-child, and he was sprinkled with water and named Biorn after his father's father. But the Queen lived not long, but died

15

the third year after this; and when the lad was but five
winters old, then was King Olaf his father fallen down
dead of a sudden, where he sat at ale-drinking in his hall.
And it was the talk of men that there was venom in the
cup, and that that was the bane of King Olaf. So he
was laid in howe at Upsala. Thereafter was Eric taken
for sole King in Sweden, and he brought up the lad and
put him to fostering with Earl Wolf, his mother's
brother. No children of King Eric born in wedlock
were as then alive, and his wife now ten years dead.
Dearly he loved his brother's son, and tendered him as he
had been his own bairn. And the lad waxed up the
goodliest to look on and strongest and likeliest of lads,
tall and great-sinewed beyond his years. And because
the lad was somewhat grim and stubborn of will and
hasty and sudden of anger and very fierce and proud,
even now in his tender youth, King Eric let lengthen his
name and let call him Styrbiorn.

Against the coming of winter, when Styrbiorn was
now fifteen winters old, Eric the King made great
blood-offering in the temple at Upsala for the goodness
of the year, as was his wont and the wont of his fathers
before him from time immemorial. Thither were come
together lords and great men of account from up and
down the land, and there was great drinking toward.
But Styrbiorn came not to meat that day, and came not
to the King's hall. So the King sent men to seek for
Styrbiorn. In a while they returned, and a man of the
King's bodyguard said, "So it is, Lord, that we found

him sitting on his father's howe, King Olaf Biornson's."

The King's brow darkened. He said to Earl Wolf, "Must this thing be, every autumn feast of sacrifice? Well, 'tis now the third time and the last; and yet it goeth nigh to anger me. Or will he not swallow my plighted word, that I will give him all, but not until he be sixteen year old?"

"I looked not for this again, King," said the Earl. "And truly I'm sorry for it."

The King made them go again to bid him to the drinking. But back they came empty-handed. "Did he answer you naught?" asked the King.

At that, they were silent, looking one at the other. Then answered one for them all and said, "Naught, Lord, save this: that he would waste no breath on the King's thralls."

"Like as his father was," said the King, "so is this young whelp. Go thou, Earl, if that might fetch him."

Earl Wolf stood up and went betwixt the benches and the fires and forth of the main door into the King's garth, and forth of the garth past the houses of men and the Thing-stead and the temple till he was come to the open field. It was murk and wild weather, and evening drawing in. Like a high house in bigness, Olaf's howe reared against the fading light. It was all overgrown with rank grass, and the tufts and tussocks of the grass ducked and paled and rose and ducked again, slapped this way and that by the blustering squalls that charged and paused and swept again about the howe, ceaselessly as the ceaseless rush of vapours in the iron-gray windy lift of the sky overhead.

Styrbiorn sat on the top of the howe, unmoved as it, face to the wind. The Earl came up to him, fain to steady himself with a hand at whiles, what with the sudden squalls and the slippery grass. When he was up, "This is ill doing," he said, shouting in his ear.

Styrbiorn moved not at all. He was muffled in a close-woven mantle of woollen stuff dyed purple and worked with black threads at the border in rich designs. Close as he held it about him, it puffed and flapped like a ship's sail in a storm when the rudder is broken. His head was bare, and the thick short curled yellow hair on it leapt to the wind's piping like the grass on the howe. He wore a heavy collar of pure gold, soft and bent to lie about his throat where neck and shoulder join, and worked by the goldsmith's art with rich enchasements, and a dragon's head at either end. He sat with his chin in his hands, frowning up-wind so that his eyes watered.

The Earl sat down and put an arm about him. "The King withholdeth not thine inheritance, Styrbiorn. He hath promised, and he will give it thee, as well thou knowest. But time is not yet. Thou art yet but fifteen winters old."

Styrbiorn shook him rudely off. "Little men's redes, foster-father, shall not serve my turn. 'Tis not in my blood." He spoke, as was ever the way of him, with a little stuttering here and there, as if the great and eager spirit of him in its haste tripped and stumbled over the slowness of his speech.

"No jot less of that blood," answered the Earl, shouting in his ear for the wind sake, "runneth in thine uncle's veins. He loveth thee. Wilt thou bite the hand that feeds thee? Go in with me. Or why needest thou put that shaming on free men, to put the name of thrall upon them?"

Styrbiorn leapt up a-laughing. "Did Aki's nose swell at that?" he cried. "Of age, saidst thou! Come off, and back me."

"Hold," said the Earl. But the lad was away: three bounds down the steep to the rough pasture, and away toward the King's hall. Earl Wolf was a handy man, but he scarce overtook him in the great hall door.

Lamps were kindled in the hall, and the ruddy firelight mingling with their colder beams pulsed and flickered, betwixt rush-strewn floor and the uncertain darkness of the roof-timbers, on bench and board and the many-coloured raiment of that great company and worshipful that there were set. Eric the King sat in his high seat on the upper bench. That other on the lower bench over against him was empty. He wore a Greek cloak of scarlet silken stuff and a blue kirtle done about with needle-work. Gold rings that weighed twelve ounces each were on his arms above the elbows, and a crown of fine gold was on his head. King Eric was of all men the fairest to look on; and for all he was well nigh three-score winters old he was neither bent nor wrinkled, but fresh-looking and stark and stalwart as any man in his prime age, and his hair and beard most fair and thick, albeit something dashed with gray, and the voice of him deep and strong and pleasant to hear, and his eyes of a gray colour and speckled, and very bright.

Styrbiorn came and stood before the King betwixt the fire and the board. The King pointed to the high seat over against him, and said, "Take thy place, kinsman."

Styrbiorn eyed him squarely, then answered and said in his hasty stuttering way, "That was in my mind, King, that I should be no more a burthen unto you nor a kept person, now that I am come to man's estate. In token whereof, I would not come to your board to-day, but abode by my father's howe."

" 'Tis wearisome," said the King, "if this old mummery must be acted anew each year. Imagine my part spoke: so, 'tis done. And now, no more on't."

Styrbiorn said, "If, King, you will do me right now. Render up to me my father's heritage: that share of the lordship of the Swedes which belonged to the King my father. Then I will sit in yonder seat. But not otherwise. Not as your guest, King."

"Kinsman," said the King, "thou art, of all folk I ever did know, man or woman, the most thrawart and stubborn of will. I say unto thee, as last year I said and the year before last: when thou shalt be sixteen winters old I will give thee thine inheritance."

"Waxed is the bairn, but not the breeks," said Styrbiorn, and his face was red as blood.

"When thou shalt be sixteen winters old," said the King. "Till then, be quiet. For stubborn-set as thou art, I am as stubborn; and I, not thou, will rule in this matter, as is but just and right."

"Seldom recovers Kings their dominions," said Styrbiorn fiercely, "but with hewing of swords." But when he had spoken those words he looked up at the King his uncle and met his gaze; and there was that in the King's countenance that stayed his violent mood, as a draught of cool water in the mouth stays the burning of an overhot mouthful of meat. There was fallen a sudden silence in the hall, for all that men were well feasted and much game and jesting was toward. And Styrbiorn, that had been red with anger, flushed yet darker even to his brow and neck; and he stood shame-faced before the King. He said in a low voice, "Some devil drew the tongue out of my mouth to speak an ill word. And now I will sit at your board, as well it befitteth I should do. But if it please you, King, I will come and talk more hereof to-morrow."

"Let us give thanks," said the King, "for a little respite."

The cup had by then gone many a time about the tables, and men's bellies were well bulked with ale and their wise discretion and judgement something befogged withal. And as in such a season a man will oft say that which tumbleth quickliest to his tongue, so Aki of

21

the King's bodyguard (bethinking him not at all that he
should as well tickle a wolf under the chin as fret Styrbiorn now) plucked him by the kirtle as he came walking by the lower bench, and asked when he should have
amends for the scurvy words Styrbiorn that day had given
him.

"Hold thy tongue, King's thrall," said Styrbiorn; and,
with the word, cast off the cloak from his shoulders and
smothered it over Aki's head. Now Aki had in his hand
a great silver-rimmed drinking-horn all full of ale, and
it spilt all down the neck of him. He leapt up and cast
away the cloak and drave the horn at Styrbiorn's nose
so that the blood gushed out of his nose and he staggered
back and well nigh into the fire. Aki ran out, but Styrbiorn overtook him in the doorway and caught him by
the collar and jerked him backwards. Young as he was,
Styrbiorn had yet the strength of an ordinary man full-
grown. He was mad wroth, and he drove the man
down under him with fist and knee. Aki had by now
pulled out a sax-knife and aimed to smite him withal.
Styrbiorn rived it out of his hand and drove it into Aki's
neck and down into the man's body, clean up to the heft
of the knife. Aki needed no other blow but was dead
at once.

Now was turmoil in the King's hall, and much carp-
ing and high talk this way and that; for Aki was a man
of good kin among the bonders, and many were there
who would have done vengeance for him on Styrbiorn
without more ado, but that the place and the King's

majesty put them in awe. In the end was all quiet again, and the dead corpse carried out, and men fell again to drinking, yet something less blithely than afore.

The next morning was Styrbiorn up betimes and betook him once more toward his father's howe. For, albeit he was well agreed with the King his uncle after last night's doings to sit quiet yet another year and thereafter be received into kingdom, yet him-seemed there should be no place where he should be more at ease when he had naught to do than there on the howe.

There was a spring in his step as he walked. He went not straight to the howe but took a sweep out into the open country, looking this way and that as searching for something. He was come within about a hundred paces from the howe when he espied that whereof he stood in need: a dark and shaggy body, four-legged, sturdy, high-shouldered, tailless, with a marvellous long and hairy coat that trailed well nigh to the big cloven hooves of the beast, and with great curly horns like a ram's, and hairy face and nose, grazing some way off from him in the rough pastures that went down to Fyriswater. Styrbiorn halted on his way and gave a low call. The thing stopped grazing, lifted head and looked and saw him. It stood still at gaze: he called again. It lifted its nose and gave an answering bellow; then, like a coyly playful girl that will be wooed but must provoke, turned about and walked away from him, casting a look behind every four or five paces to make sure it was being fol-

lowed. Styrbiorn was upon it ere it had gone twenty
yards, and caught it by the horns. "Moldi," he said,
"how durst thou, when I want thee?" It was a yearling
musk-ox, littler than common oxen, but heavy enough
and strong enough to do with most men as it would; but
with Styrbiorn, as was well seen as they tussled and
strove together, it was very nicely matched. Round
and round they swung for a while, trampling the ground,
swaying and staggering back and forth, puffing and
snorting both the one and the other, till Styrbiorn broke
off the game and leaped backward several paces and there
stood panting and laughing, facing his little ox. "Come
on," he shouted; and it put down its head and charged.
Styrbiorn braced his whole frame to bear the onset, and
by the sheer strength of him stood his ground. This
bout they played over not twice nor thrice but a dozen
times; wherein three times was Styrbiorn thrown, but
all other times he was victor in their encounter. But
whenever Styrbiorn was thrown, his little ox was careful
not to trample nor hurt him, but shoved its nose into his
face, breathing its sweet breath all about him, and then
stood back for the charge as soon as he was gotten on his
feet again. At length they stopped both. Styrbiorn
sat on the ground propped on his two hands behind him,
breathing hard. Moldi stood over him, nuzzling his
hairy nose into Styrbiorn's neck between jaw and collar-
bone. Styrbiorn rubbed his cheek on Moldi's nose like
a cat. In a minute he stood up. "To the howe," he
said. Moldi turned and set off the contrary way. Styr-

biorn caught him, and with less violent tussling now,
(for they were now both well blown and desired no
longer sinew-testing in earnest but some show of it only
to mind them of their sport), half dragged half coaxed
him to the howe. There they rested together an hour or
more, the one fitting heads to his arrows, the other chewing the cud. A mile or more eastward, on their left,
rose the scree-slopes of Windbergsfell: southaway from
beneath their feet wound Fyriswater amid the flats below
Upsala, and there lay spread the far-stretching low
country toward Sigtun and the sea, and westward the far
mountains of Upland shadowy-gray in the light of
morning.

When Moldi had taken his fill of chewing the cud,
he stood up and butted Styrbiorn gently from behind.
Styrbiorn sprang up and caught him by the horns, and
again they fought and wrastled on the howe top, till
Styrbiorn forced Moldi's head round sideways and threw
him down and held him there by main force, his face
against his. A long time they lay so, Moldi ever and
again putting forth spasmodic efforts to rise, Styrbiorn
holding him down with all his might and laughing the
while in his brown and furry ear.

At length Moldi lay quiet, as if to grant he was mastered as for this time. Styrbiorn let go, and rolled over
on his back. His eyes were closed, his great and shapely
arms flung out a-stretch on either side, his right hand
burrowing and fondling among the warm soft depths of
woolly hair under Moldi's jowl, his left opening and

shutting as if to ease the stiffness in his fingers after so
much clutching on the horns.   His chest, broad and deep
as few men's of full age, mounted and sank with slow
regular and profound breaths.   So he lay, with shut eyes
and with lips parted a little like a dreamer's who smiles
in his sleep; and all the while knew not who was stolen
up quietly behind him on the howe, and had all the while
stood there looking down on that rough and tumble, the
hard panting of boy and ox, the splendour of Styrbiorn's
strong limbs with every sinew strained and hard in the
struggle: and stood there still, watching him in silence.

A tall lass she was, standing there over him, her dark
gown gathered in one hand so that her shapely ankles
showed below it.   Her hair, tawny red, braided with
gold cords into two thick trammels, reached to her knee
at either side.   High-bosomed she was, light of flank,
clean-limbed, and with somewhat of almost manly presence and stature, yet graceful beyond all telling.   The
carriage of her was like the dragon-head of a ship of
war treading turbulent seas, and the face of her (albeit
she was yet scarce grown woman), of that kind and
seeming which belike Queen Brynhild's had of old, or
Gudrun's of Laxriverdale, and other women's faces that
were born to be the bane of men.

But this was not the lady Gudrun come from Iceland, nor yet Brynhild, Budli's daughter, returned from
her Hell-ride in these latter days and back from the dead,
that stood with proud grave mouth and unsounded dark-
brown eyes gazing on the might of Styrbiorn while he

struggled with Moldi on his father's howe; but Sigrid, Skogul-Tosti's daughter out of Arland, the mightiest and noblest of all men of Sweden who lacked title of dignity, and she some few days since ridden from home with her father for feasting and guesting with King Eric Biornson.

Opening his eyes at last and seeing her, Styrbiorn sat up a little sullen-looking and shame-faced and gave her greeting. He gave Moldi a flick on the nose with the back of his hand, who forthwith lumbered up to his feet and down from the howe and away.

"This is a strange sport," said Sigrid. "What manner of cow is this?"

" 'Tis not a cow," said Styrbiorn. " 'Tis my bull. He cometh from the northlands, many days' journey beyond Helsingland. His name is Moldi."

He began tinkering again with his arrows, fitting heads to them. Sigrid watched, bending over his shoulder from behind. Styrbiorn took no more note of her than if she had been his musk-ox. "Shall I sit here awhile?" she said at length.

"As thou wilt," answered he.

Sigrid sat down beside him with the grace of a sea-bird alighting on the wave. His shoulder was turned towards her. He went on with his work. Herself unobserved, she sat there quiet, looking on what he did, but most on him.

"Arrows is women's weapons," said Styrbiorn after a while, looking along the shaft to see he had fitted it true.

"I know not why I fash myself with such things."

Sigrid said nothing, watching the ripple of the muscles beneath his skin of arms and neck and shoulder, the great clean-modelled knees, and the yellow hair of his head so close and thick.

"It is a wonder thou shouldst like to sit all by thyself in this place," she said.

He made no answer. She was so near that the breath of her, sweet like kine's breath, mixed with his own.

"There be few men so strong as to hold down that bull," said she.

"He getteth me down now and then," said Styrbiorn.

Sigrid's shoulder touched his, lightly as a moth. He shifted away a little, laying down one arrow and choosing another. She shifted too, the other way. Her face flamed red on a sudden, and turned fierce and hard so as it was a wonder to see in a girl so young and tender. For a long time they were silent. Then she said, "I did never see a man slain till last night."

"Wast afeared to see it?" asked Styrbiorn.

"Not afeared," she said. "Thou hast ta'en to the work young." She was looking at him somewhat strangely, her eyes a-sparkle.

"I slew him not sackless," said Styrbiorn. " 'Would have stabbed me first. Thou knewest that?"

"I knew it truly," she answered.

"And I'll pay no boot for his slaying," said Styrbiorn, turning to look her in the eye. "I'll learn these bonders' sons to bear them more quietly in kings' houses," said he.

She said nothing.

"It is good to be a king," said Styrbiorn after a little.

Sigrid seemed as if she heard him not. She was gazing with an altered countenance south over Fyrisfield. Styrbiorn looked up and saw her so stare, wide-eyed, as if in fear: as if in those silent water-meadows she saw some strange matter, hidden until now.

"Wouldst not thou be a queen, Sigrid," said he, "and 'twere offered thee?"

Still she spoke not. A cloud in that instant hid the sun. The girl shivered.

"Wouldst thou not?" said Styrbiorn.

"Not what?" said she, shivering again and turning to look at him. "I marked not what thou saidst."

"Be a queen?" said Styrbiorn.

"Yes," she said.

"Why dost thou look so, as if thou hadst seen something?"

" 'Tis nothing," she said. But seeing in his eyes that her looks belied her words, "Nothing," said she again. "Thou art but a child, Styrbiorn, for all that thou didst slay a man last night."

"Something too childishly," said he, scowling, "goeth mine affair. It needed not thee too, to thrust that down my throat."

Sigrid shivered and said, "Come from this place. I

am three years older than thou, and can see things thou canst not see. The dead be in this place. Come away."

But Styrbiorn budged not from his seat. He took another arrow, then smiling scornfully said to her, "Thou art a woman, Sigrid. Women are ever afeared of bugs and bogles. The living be in this place: thou and I: not the dead. And well I love this place. 'Tis a place of Kings. And if any dead man be hereabout, it is the King my father."

He looked up at her again. Her eyes were fixed on him, but as if she saw him not. She looked ghastly. He leaped up and took her by the arm, being bit with remorse a little for his churlishness, and a little touched with the infection of her strange speechless dread; even as it is a man of rare coolness, who, sitting alone with his dog in a desolate house at night-time, seeth the dog stare and growl as if at some unseen presence in the room and feeleth in himself no answering tremor. "Come," he said, "I'll go in with thee. There's naught to fear. Come."

II

Thorgnyr the Lawman

NOW there was mighty discontent among the bonder-folk because of this slaying of Aki, and much murmuring against Styrbiorn and his lawless and unbridled vein who should so slay the man and pay no boot therefor. In the end the King himself did boot it, and so these growls died down for the while.

When it was spring, the King fared north into the coasted parts of Helsingland and into Jarnberaland a-guesting, and it was full summer when he came home, riding with them of his bodyguard down to the high arm of the firth over against Sigtun. It was a windy day of driving mist that made gray and ghostly the whole face of the country-side, blotting out the hills and woods and confounding water and sky in the same hue and tone of pale grey without colour; only the water was darkened with the little shadows innumerable of the hastening waves, and here and there a reef showed, darker than aught else visible, and against it the flash of breakers that leapt and fell. Like swooping birds, black squalls swooped and chased one another, scurrying in zigzags far and wide, doubling and turning, always with little glass-smooth strips of calm water on the edges of the squalls. And there were swift changing markings made by the wind and tide, as it were a white sword and a black that crossed edges on the troubled surface of the loch. A man on a dark horse came riding up from the water-side to meet the King. The King knew him for Earl Wolf.

"Thy colour looketh trouble," said the King. "What's the tidings?"

The Earl told him in his ear, as one who disburdeneth himself of a weighty matter and a grievous and feareth the while lest evil betide him, as sometimes it betideth to those who tell bad news to kings. A pretty tale in truth the Earl had to tell: of a Thing summoned in Upsala against all law, the King being not there; and at the Thing fierce disputes betwixt the bonder-folk of the one part and Styrbiorn and his friends of the other, with all the grief of Aki's slaying dug up anew and all their old counts against Styrbiorn, wherein at last Styrbiorn said loudly that he was, of his father's right, King of half the realm of Sweden, and they should learn it to their cost. Whereupon, great uproar among the bonders, who in fine carried it with so high a hand that they feared not to choose and proclaim one Lambi the White, a man from Stocksound in Tenthland, King in Styrbiorn's despite of that half of the kingdom claimed by him; and therewith the Thing broken up in a tumult, so that it had wanted but a little to have befallen a battle betwixt the King's men and the bonders.

The King heard him out, and was silent for a little space, his countenance clouded. At length, "It agreeth i' the main," said he, "with that which I knew hereof already."

34

"You did already know?" said the Earl, much wondering.

"Many are the King's ears. Was Thorgnyr not there to stop them when they made this fair election?" asked the King.

"There was he, it is most certain," said Earl Wolf. "But he did little enough to stop them."

"I do trust Thorgnyr in all things else," said the King, "but not in aught that toucheth Styrbiorn. He hath been ever against him."

The Earl was silent.

"Was Thorgnyr there," asked the King, "whenas they fell a-pelting of you with stones and muck to drive you from the Thing, thee and Styrbiorn?"

"You did know that too, King?" said the Earl. "I did think to have told you that later, not to light in a moment too hot a fire of anger in you. And yet, a pretty scout; a pretty shaming. 'Twere well to engrave the memory of those stones on the skin-coat of some of 'em."

"Thou'st not yet answered me," said King Eric: "was Thorgnyr in it when they stoned you from the Thing?"

"Lord, I'll not lie to you," answered the Earl; "he was not. O' the contrary, I am apt to think that Thorgnyr, i' the midst o' this pother, was like naught so much as an unhandy cook, who, when he had brewed him this kettle full of trouble, did sit it over the fire until it boil, and did find too late he had not power

35

in's lean scragged arms to lift it off again afore all the
mess should bubble over."

"I must see Thorgnyr," said the King. "Hast thou
a boat here to put us across to Sigtun?"

The Earl brought him down to the water and showed
him three ships, enough to take the King and all his
company. They two stood together on the bank while
the King's men embarked. Earl Wolf looked angry as
a man might be, biting of his moustachios and spitting
out the hairs. The King, so long as he thought good,
let him abide in this taking; then, wearying of the entertainment, "Let not fear shut thy mouth," he said.
"If I will hear Thorgnyr, how much more thee, which
art blameless in this matter?"

"Have my thanks, King, for that," said the Earl.
"He is thy dog, I'll not gainsay it. But here, where
it toucheth Styrbiorn, will you see Thorgnyr? Will
you hear this? How? this Lambi, this man of naught,
this scurvy shagrag, chosen and proclaimed (flatly
'gainst the law) joint King in your noble young kinsman's room? and will you see Thorgnyr? will you
bandy words with him?"

"Why wilt thou make such faces?" said the King.

"It was not so in Sweden aforetime," said Earl Wolf,
in a hot anger fanned by the breath of his own angry
speech. "Did not King Ingiald Evil-heart formerly
burn six kings in Upsala, 'cause he would have no man
share his dominion? Can you for shame——" but here
he came to a full stop in his declaiming, having not so

36

wholly suffered his indignation to master his sober senses
that he should not mark that look in the King's eye suddenly turned upon him, and be cowed by it to sub-
mission.

"To shame at that which is not shameworthy," said
the King after a minute, very quiet, "belongeth to a
fool, not to a king. And thou, that hast been a famous
skipper in thy time! Ay," said the King: "that was
well thought on. Yonder little cock-boat shall serve."
That was a little boat some fifteen foot long, that went
with one of the big ships; and the King made the Earl
go aboard of her and put off, they two alone. The
King made Earl Wolf sit in the stern and steer, and
made him hoist sail and steer for Sigtun. "Now I will
see somewhat of thy seamanship," said the King.

The Earl sailed handily, keeping his course as near
as man could in that stormy weather; but ever and
again, struck broadside by a charging squall, he must
slack sail or throw her head into the wind.

"Is it as I think?" said the King, "that thy prac-
tice agreeth not with thy so loud babble? Make fast
the sheet and keep her on a straight course to Sigtun, or
it shall go ill with thee." Nor would he harken at all
to the Earl's protestings, but threatened him with a
great spear with an iron head a foot long; so that the
Earl obeyed, and in a moment the boat was swamped
and both King and Earl thrown into the water.

When they that were by the ships saw this they were
put in a mighty stew and ran out a row-boat, but both

King and Earl swam strongly and were come ashore
before those others were well started out to rescue them.
The King shook himself like a dog and fell a-laughing
with great shouts of laughter. He clapped Earl Wolf
on the shoulder, who stood there as a man not well
knowing whether to laugh or be cross, wringing the
water out of his breeches and kirtle. "Let me alone to
rule Sweden," said the King; "and do thou thy part
to lesson thy foster-son with good and wholesome rede.
And learn him not thy fashion of seamanship, but mine.
For certain it is, there's no shore to swim to, as here,
whenas kingdoms are overset."

Thorgnyr Thorgnyrson the Lawman came that same
evening, obedient to the sending of Eric the King, to
hold talk with him in a little fire-hall where the King
was wont to sit when he would be private. The King
made Thorgnyr sit on a low stool before the King's
feet. Old of years was Thorgnyr, and his beard both
long and white, and his brow much furrowed, and with
great shaggy eyebrows obscuring his eyes, and his cheeks
hollow and lined, and his nose like an eagle's beak. The
head of him was bald.

The King said, "Fowls and beasts which herdeth
and flocketh: is it to this pass thou wilt bring me the
Swede-realm, Thorgnyr?"

Thorgnyr looked at him in silence for a moment.
Then he answered and said, "To be free with you, King

'tis a younger than I and a nearer your own blood you should abraid with these unfortunes, not me."

"So," said the King: "sith old men's hands grow feeble and let fall authority, we are to blame it on young blood that it runneth strong? We were best geld our young men, think'st thou, to make 'em docile, so as we may live out our time in quiet? or expose 'em all, and breed up girl-children only, that I and thou in our dotage may still find obedience?"

Thorgnyr bowed his head. "I marvel not, Lord, if you be angry. But if I wrought not my best for your interest so far as in me lay, then ask I no further thing at your hands than the loss of all I can lose: goods, lands, liberty, and last my life withal."

"By whose authority," said the King, "was this assembly holden, when the Thing was broken up according to law and I gone otherwhere for a season?"

"There was no authority for it, Lord," answered he.

"Was it thy doing, Thorgnyr?" said the King.

He answered, "No."

"Was it against thy strong withstanding?" said the King again.

"Lord, you must not press me over hard," said Thorgnyr. "It was neither by my will nor counsel: that I can surely swear unto you."

The King sat very still. Then he said, not raising his tone, yet with a note in his voice that menaced like a great dog's growl, low and dangerous, "Is it come to this, that it must be tried out at last whether I or the bonders hath the lordship of this land of Sweden?"

The old man was silent, staring into the fire.

"I will have thine answer," said the King.

Slowly Thorgnyr turned and looked in the King's face. "Then answer me my question, King: Whether with the sun or with the rain ripeneth the corn unto harvest?"

Chin in hand, the King leaned over the arm of his carven chair, studying that old man where he sat bent in the dancing fire-light, one pale fine hand tight-clutched across the other shoulder, holding close about him the gathered folds of his cloak of minivere, as if even by that hot fire his lean body was a-cold, the other clenched on his knee. After a while the King began to say, "Thou and I wax old. And when we are laid in howe the ordering of these things shall lie in other men's hands, and they will order them as the Fates shall ordain. Belike it were a wise man's part to let alone: what must be must be. Yet is that not my way. And besides, Thorgnyr," said the King in an altered voice, "I do love this lad."

After a pause, "Thou art silent," said the King. "What dost think on?"

"Must I tell you, Lord?"

"Thou must," said the King.

For a minute, Thorgnyr abode silent. Then, "This it is, then," answered he: "that Styrbiorn's stout stomach shall likely undo both he himself and us."

"Pshaw!" said the King, "thou'rt jaūndiced. Thou seest all yellow."

"Say rather, Lord," replied Thorgnyr, "that were a blind goose that knew not a fox from a fern-bush. At this Thing, ill as it was that it should have come to such a pass, I could have smoothed all, but by his row and ruckling was all upsy-turvy turned, and the Thing broke up in an uproar. He first set the ball flying, and returned 'em gibe for gibe and fierce word for fierce word."

The King said menacingly, "They stoned my kinsman and my Earl, I am let to know."

"I could not help it," said Thorgnyr. And he paused. "Will you suffer me to speak plain, Lord?"

The King said, "Speak."

"You have known the truth of my mind these forty year and more. And afore that, my father served the King your father, and counselled him faithfully with wholesome counsel. Truly I say unto you, King, the Swede-folk will not abear to be spur-ridden; and most unbearable shall be the spurrings of this young man."

"And I," said King Eric, swinging round on him in a flash of anger, "will not abear false kings i' the land."

"If you will take my rede, Lord," said Thorgnyr, quailing not at all, "you will be so high-minded as, eagle-like, to disdain this little fowl. I swear to you I had no part in it, but stay them then I could not. 'Twas done in a hot folly of rage, under what stress of provo-

cation you do know. It will die out like a spark, unless you, Lord, by untimely blowing on't should puff it to
flame indeed."

"I," said the King, "tread down sparks, not blow 'em,
whenso I've a mind to put 'em out. The bonders
know me, and I them. If I reach not out mine hand
now upon this Lambi they will not mistake the reason;
nor he neither, if he have wit. Bid him keep quiet,
or safest depart out of the land. Thou hast ways and
means: see to it, thou. Styrbiorn I will send abroad
for three years, furnishing his depart with both ships
and men sufficient for notable doings if, as I think, he
hath the parts to use them. So shall he redden tooth
somewhat otherwise than on mine own men here in
Sweden, and after three years come home ripe to be received into kingdom."

"You plant well, King," said Thorgnyr, shaking his
head. "Pray Gods the mould prove not barren and
unapt."

A man of the King's bodyguard came in and louting
before the King asked would he see Styrbiorn. The
King bade admit him straight. Styrbiorn came swiftly
in, saw Thorgnyr, and came to a full stop betwixt the
carved jambs of the doorway. He looked from the
King to Thorgnyr, from Thorgnyr to the King. His
face grew grim and the hair of his head was raised a
little, like the heckles of a savage dog in the presence
of an enemy. "It is the worst of shames," said he, "if
you, Lord, will discourse thus friendly with that old

42

man. Let lead him out and hew him before the doors; that were a good deed."

The King gazed sternly at him, but spake no word.

"Lord," said Styrbiorn, standing still in the doorway in the light of the fire, "I came to ask a boon of you. And this it is, that you find me twenty ships, Lord, and suffer me go a-harrying. And give me leave too to slay your outlaw Lambi the White, which these shagamuffin bonders and that old man did openly name for king. And that was the biggest shame ever heard tell of."

Thorgnyr's eyes were bent on the young man from under their deep-jutting eaves. His face was calm and his brow unruffled, but none might see the eyes of him watching from those dark sockets where the fitful fire-light never pierced.

"Kinsman," said King Eric, "thou art young. Therefore at thine injustice and want of judgment I wonder not: years and knowledge shall mend it. For the rest, not twenty but sixty ships shalt thou have, and a full tale of men thereto, and it is my will that thou be three winters abroad. There shalt thou, being king-born, learn the trade of kings. After that, if out of so many and great scapes thou come back safe and sound, I think I shall find thee a man grown, and a right son of thy father's, and a right kinsman of mine. And that shall be the best day of all my life's days, when I shall receive thee in thy father's stead, joint King with me in Upsala."

43

When the King his uncle had so spoken, Styrbiorn's face put off in an instant his fierce and dogged look and he looked upon the King with so open and merry a smile as must have made even an ill-willer wish to love him, and his hair bristled no more but lay down as it should upon his head. He came forward into the room.

"As for this Lambi," said the King, "he is naught: a fly: a gob of spittle: I regard him not at all. I forbid thee, on thy life, to fight with him in Sweden or the coasts thereof. But if ye hap together in the outlands or on the main seas, why, let it befall as Fate shall will."

"King," answered Styrbiorn, "you have nobly dealt with me. And I swear to abide by all you bid me."

The King said, "I will now that ye twain be friends, thou and Thorgnyr. I will you to handsel friendship to each other, here in this place."

Thorgnyr held out his hand; but Styrbiorn paused, then stepped a pace backward. "I'll give him my hand," he said, "when I can give it with a good will. Another day."

"Well," said Thorgnyr, "at least I love open honesty."

"The lad hath been sore tried," said the King when Styrbiorn was gone. "I do see greatness in him."

Thorgnyr looked at the King from the inscrutable dark of his deep-thatched eye-sockets. "Ay, Lord," he said. "But the end tries all."

44

III

Queen Sigrid the Haughty

STYRBIORN now fared abroad according to the King's command. And summer wore, and winter, and when winter was well past King Eric came south to Arland to guest with Skogul-Tosti, the father of that Sigrid who was with Styrbiorn on King Olaf's howe, and saw visions there as is aforesaid. Tosti was a great friend of the King's, and made him noble entertainment; and when the King had sat there three days with his folk that were with him Tosti prayed him sit another three, and when those were done he prayed him yet three days more, so that nine days all told they feasted it in Tosti's hall.

Skogul-Tosti was a portly man and a stately, and the most open handed of men in all things which belong to housekeeping, and a showy man in his dress. It liked him better that his worthiness should call him to that reputation, to be the greatest man in all the country-side he might overlook from his home-mead at Hawkby, rather than he should exercise larger dominion over lands and folk and yet be called but the King's man, and the tool of a greatness not his own. He was the greatest of warriors, and spent much time a-warring. His wife was named Gudrid. She was a stirring woman, of the kin of the Earls of West Gautland. She was fair to look on, but folk deemed her over proud and grasping and somewhat hard of heart.

At this ninth night of their feast, when men had well eaten and were fallen now to jesting and story-telling and drinking one to another, the King spake and said, "Early it is, and yet, Tosti, I will drink no more, except thy daughter Sigrid bear cup to me."

Sigrid was set on the cross-bench on the dais, beside her mother, and the other women-folk that were at the feast sat out away from them on either hand. She had a gown of blue, collared and purfled with mink's fur, and about the neck of it sets of gold, in every set four pieces of amber. And she had above her brow a fillet of silk and twisted wire of gold, to keep back from her face the red deep masses of her hair, that came down in two thick and heavy trammels or plaits beside her bosom on either hand, and the ends tucked up under her jewelled belt.

Tosti, from his high-seat on the lower bench, called her by name and said, "Why dally, Sigrid? Are we become so slack as keep our guests waiting? and much more when 'tis the King."

She, glancing with her dark eyes first in her father's face then in the King's, reached out her hand now to the great golden drinking horn which a thrall, obedient to her father's nod, proffered to her full of mead so that the foam of it ran down the sides. As a ship's mast, half laid over by a gust of wind, rises erect from the trough of the wave, so rose she, and with modest and downward look came past the benches till she was stood beside the King.

48

King Eric took the horn with one hand and the lady with the other, and made her sit beside him in the high seat. From this she at first hung aback, but he would have his way. She sat here very demure, answering but ay or no or with a flickering smile to whatso the King might say to her: very quiet and estranged. So, and in such a quietness, Sigrid sat in the high seat beside the King; till the fires burned low, and men's eyelids waxed heavy, and it was late night, and the feast was done.

"This is what thou hast long set thy mind on," said Skogul-Tosti to his wife at his coming to bed, "and I think thou mayst be glad at this night's work."

"So far, good," said she. "But the ship's not beached yet."

"Not beached yet? Beached it is, and laid up," said Tosti. "Thou shalt see, ere the King ride hence to-morrow he will bespeak her in marriage for Styrbiorn."

"That will be well so far," said she.

"Well? what better?" Tosti, that was sat taking off his shoes, stared wonderingly up in his wife's smiling and doubting face. "And by thy good schemings he and she have been good friends together too."

"She hath said no to a dozen ere now, and not one of them but had been a great match such as should do us honour. Hast forgot how thy young messmate fared, Harald the Grenlander? and he is a king now."

"True enough," said he. "The lass hath a stubborn will, that is true. And her very scornfulness and

49

haughty ways seem to draw 'em on, only to send 'em packing. But there's bigger game on the wing here."

"That is true, too," said Gudrid. "But, remember: thou'st a wayward daughter."

"A right daughter of thine, mistress. As skittish as an eel." Gudrid laughed. "But she hath wit," he said: "she can lick a dish before a cat. She'll ne'er say nay to Styrbiorn."

"I say only this," said Gudrid: "be not too certain sure."

" 'Tis a wonder past guessing," said Tosti, standing up, "all these doubts and questions of thine. Hast spoke to her on't?"

"No," said she. "But I watched her. She smelt well enough what was toward to-night. I liked not the face she put on it."

"But not say no to this? There's no higher game to fly at."

Gudrid shook her head. " 'Tis thy giving of her her will too much, and cockering of her. She'd ne'er mind me, and now not thee neither."

"Well," said Tosti, "she shall have her will, too, whatsome'er she choose. Albeit, I'll ne'er believe she'd say nay to this."

Gudrid said nothing, but stood looking at him as on some new and entertaining thing. He, knowing not what to make of her and her looks, took her by the shoulders. "She hath this of thee," he said, "that she is like to be an ill curse to any man save the man of her

own choosing." And he drew his wife to him and
kissed her on the neck and bare shoulder.

Next morning the King took Tosti apart and said to
him, "There is a matter I have to move unto thee, Tosti,
and I think after last night it will not take thee nap-
ping. And it toucheth thy daughter Sigrid."

Tosti answered, "Your drift, Lord, is not hidden
from me, and I do embrace it for the greatest honour
and gladness that ever did or could befall me and my
kindred. Yet since true is that which is said, 'There's
many a thing in the carle's cot that is not in the king's
garth,' and since this is mine only daughter, I know
you will not take it ill, Lord, if I leave unto her the
choosing in this. So have I alway done heretofore,
and so it seemeth me will be best now, both for her
and for all that have part herein."

"I will talk to her myself," said the King. "None
did yet die of another's wound, nor should any be content with another's choosing."

The King walked with Sigrid forth beyond the home-
mead by sheep-ways on to the open fell-sides south
toward Balingsdale. For a long while he was
silent. Then suddenly he said, "I have a suit unto thee,
Sigrid."

"That is not hard to guess, Lord," said she, dreaming
not that the King had any other purpose than this,
whereof she had long since had an inkling in her
parents' minds, to wed her and Styrbiorn.

"What answer," said the King, "must I have of thee?"

Sigrid, looking straight before her, replied, "I will tell you, Lord, if you will tell me first whether it resteth in my free choice to say yes or no to you."

"Thy father," said King Eric, "hath laid all in thine hand, to answer as thou shalt please. Besides, I would take no other answer."

"Then, Lord," said she, "my answer is No."

At that, the King stopped short. Sigrid too stopped and faced him. Her face was very red. "I must have thy reason," said the King.

She made no answer.

The King said, "I will put no stress on thee, Sigrid. But as well as I am minded to entreat thee, surely so well it befitteth thee to answer me and tell me thy reasons. For this match is not as another, which haply thy high mind might not think honourable enough for thee."

Still for a minute she faced the King in silence. Very proud she looked, her brown eyes deep and unsearchable like a deer's; then her eyes dropped and she turned away. "I see," said the King: "this hath come over sudden upon thee."

Sigrid laughed. "Nay, Lord, 'tis but the old tale again, the old song." And she began to say:

> I ken a verse:
> An eagle sat upon a stane!
> And I ken another:
> An eagle sat upon a stane!

And I ken a third:
An eagle sat upon a stane!
The first is like 'em all:
An eagle sat upon a stane!

She looked up at him, an angry, mocking look. The King's face hardened. She threw out her hands, and, "What can a maid do withal," said she, "if men do so plague her? Must I take this untried boy because he is come of kingly blood? and because he hath the King to come a-wooing for him? And truly," she said, turning her head away, "I do hold Styrbiorn no better than a cat's son."

King Eric stared: then, seeing which way the wind set, he brake out a-laughing and reached out and took her by the hand. "Why, here's a pretty diversion," said he, "of cross questions and crooked answers. I will woo thee, Sigrid, for no man's hand but mine own. And this is my suit to thee, to be mine own wedded wife, and Queen in Upsala."

Her hand yet in the King's hand, her body poised in free proud lines like the wild birches, daughters of the fell and the free elements, Sigrid stood very still. Her breathing was quickened. After a while the King said, "And now, what answer wilt thou give me?"

They had halted by the margin of a tarn, part thawed. The wind blowing from the far side drove the ice up on to the bank where they stood. The packing ice crackled and moaned with a soft and high-pitched moaning, and the broken bits of it tinkled in the wind-stirred water with a tinkling as of faint bells. Sigrid said, very low, "That was one answer I gave you, when I thought you did speak for Styrbiorn." Then, starting suddenly out of her quiet, she strove to withdraw her hand from the King's, but he kept it. "I pray you let me go," she cried. "You will bruise my hand." Then her face flamed red and her eyes turned hard and fierce: "Must I answer you, Lord, as to the King? or as to an old man come a-wooing?"

The King, letting go her hand indeed, caught her in his arms. She, frightened as soon as she had spoken it lest her gibe, that she could not bite in, of old man, might yet have lost her that high advancement which her soul lusted for, abode breathless in his strong embrace that taught her how empty was her gibe, and, being empty, harmless. "I will show thee," said King Eric, speaking hot and close in her ear and hair, "how thou must answer me. Thus would I have thee answer me, Sigrid, as to a great man of war that do love thee, and will not let thee go. And will not let thee go: Sigrid the Haughty."

Yet, so hard and stiff abode she in his embrace, without word spoken, that he at length did let her go. She stood back now with hands behind her, facing him steadily with those liquid eyes inscrutable. "It is well seen, Lord," said she, "that you are stronger than I. Yet remember, there be two needed for every agreement."

"That is but fair and right," said the King. "There

54

shall no constraint be put upon thee, whether of hand or word. But here in this place shalt thou choose."

She stood silent.

"Thou shalt have till to-morrow morn, then," said the King.

But still she stood silent. May be, strange and contrarious thoughts contended within her head, under the braided heaviness of tresses that flung back the weak sun's radiance in shifting flashes of red-gold fire. At length she turned full on the King those brown eyes of hers: "And which way would you have me choose, Lord?" said she.

"Which way?" said the King. "That is a strange question, and needeth no answer."

Again for a while she was silent. Her eyes were troublous to a man to behold when they looked so upon him; even as a man might voyage over an undiscovered sea, uncertain whether these were safe unplumbed depths he sailed over, or but shallow rock-strewn waters apt for his destruction. Then suddenly her eyelids flickered and her proud lips sweetened and she became all yielding loveliness. "The strong man's rede ruleth still," she said, and came to his arms.

IV

Jomsburg

PALNATOKI of Fion dwelt in those days in Jomsburg, and was captain there. A marvellous sure place had he made it, builded with stone walls about and about, and he had, in the gut of the harbour-mouth, a sea-gate like to the gate of a walled town, so as a three hundred long-ships might enter and ride in the harbour within the sea-gate. And in the castle or burg was good house-room for every man of them that was in the Lay (or, as some say, the Law) of the Jomsburgers, and treasure chambers enow to keep safe the good treasure they brought home thither from their harrying, and store chambers filled with corn and meal and kippered fish and all manner of victual and stores. And there was within that burg a well of fresh water always flowing, and both landward and seaward it was a place not to be fought against, girt about with thick high walls inexpugnable and stone cliffs washed with the sea.

There was as then with Palnatoki in Jomsburg these lords, to wit: Bui the Thick of Borgundholm and Sigurd Cape, his brother; and Biorn the Brisk; and those three sons of Strut-Harald that was in that time a famous Earl in Skaney, Sigvaldi namely and Heming and Thorkell the High; and these three were brothers-in-law to Bui and Sigurd, since Sigurd had to wife Tofa

59

the daughter of Strut-Harald. Besides these there were
in Jomsburg many lords and men of mark, and all in
their prime age and with power and means to hand with
their will; blood-suppers, every one ready to leap, like a
hand-wolf, into his natural wildness: and yet (which
indeed made the main strength and anchor of their
state) every one ready to leave, in all things of matter,
the whole regiment of that burg and host with Palnatoki.

For every man of them, were he of great estate or
were he least among their fellowship, must swear a
strong oath to hold by the lay of the Jomsburgers. And
therein were these things covenanted:

First, that there should no man be received in that
fellowship older than fifty nor any younger than eighteen winters. Nor yet any that would run from another of like strength and like-weaponed with himself.
And thirdly, that every man of them should be sworn
to avenge another's slaying, as though he were his own
brother. Fourthly, that none should kindle slander
among men there. Fifth, though they should take to
a man which had slain father or brother of one that
was already there before him, or a kinsman of his, if
that came to light after their taking to him, then should
the whole award and settlement of this lie with Palnatoki. Also, whatsoever of tidings might thither come,
none should be so hardy as tell aught thereof, seeing
that it was for Palnatoki alone to tell all tidings. And
he that should be found in default touching aught of

these things aforesaid, the same should be driven away and turned out of their law. None might have a woman in the burg. Nor none might be abroad longer than three nights but by leave of Palnatoki. Whatsoever they might get with harrying they must bear it to the pole, were it much or little, so it were money's worth; and if it were shown of any man that he did not so, then must that man be put away and out of their law, were it much or little. No man might speak or utter there any craven word, howsoever hopeless a turn their affair might take. There could not anything befall within the burg of such a kind as that they themselves must shape and settle it, but Palnatoki alone must there rule all things according to his will. Nor might ties of kinship nor of friendship sway the matter if men should wish to come thither who were not in their law; no, not though at the bidding of men already there they should come thither, it no whit availed them if they were not fit.

So they sat in the burg in good peace, and kept well their laws. They fared abroad every summer a-harrying in this land and in that and gat them good fee and good renown. And they were held for the greatest champions and men of war, and scarcely was any man thought their match in that time.

Now was summer-day long past of that summer following the things in Sweden we have told of, and they of Jomsburg were home from the sea to discharge their havings and fit their ships anew, and so fare forth again

one more voyage afore winter. Palnatoki, walking betimes on the sea-wall facing the brow of dawn, beheld
ships bear down out of the main north-eastward under
oar and sail: sixty, steering for Jomsburg. There was a
land-breeze blowing, light and fitful, and the sea was
smooth under Jomsburg walls, with shags fishing and
diving and a whirl of white sea-mews screaming and
gaffling in the air above them. The ships drew near,
till they were come within ear-shot. And by then were
the most of the Jomsburgers stood on the sea-wall with
Palnatoki.

The greatest of those ships drew in nearest under the
wall. She was swart-black and fair with gold, and
her sail was striped red and blue and green. Her prow
was a drake's head scaled with black iron and scarlet-
tongued and with eyes and crest of shining gold, and
the shields that hung along her gunwale from bow to
stern were painted with many colours and studded with
bronze and iron that blinked in the growing light of
morning.

There stood on her poop a man in a blue kirtle and
a ring-byrny of iron, and helmed with an iron helm
burnished and inlaid with gold; and his helm was
winged with the wings of a buzzard erect and shadowing above either ear. So when his ship was come
over against that place whereas those lords of Jomsburg were stood together on the wall, that man ut-
tered command and the oarsmen backed and held her.
And he hailed them on the wall.

Palnatoki gave back his greeting, and asked what man was he, and what countryman.

Then answered he from the poop, "I am Styrbiorn, whom men call the Swedes' Champion, son of Olaf the Swede-King. And this is my host, and we be of the Swede-realm."

Palnatoki asked what was their errand.

Styrbiorn answered, they would have guesting there.

"This is no guest-house of Jomsburg," answered Palnatoki. "And I and my mates be no lovers of guests nor guestings."

Styrbiorn said, "To him of you that is Toki Palni's son would I talk: to thee, with the nose like an eagle; or art not thou he?"

Palnatoki answered, "I am that man."

"Ay, and 'tis a bird hath claws," cried Bui.

"We be not come hither a-begging," said Styrbiorn to Palnatoki. "Neither art thou and thine wont to beg whether fee or forbearance at other men's hands, nor yet the more am I and mine. This is mine errand: to offer you my friendship, and be with you in Jomsburg, and sail with you a-viking."

"He stuttereth," said Bui, "like a pig at the trough."

Palnatoki gazed at Styrbiorn a minute narrowly, as a skipper studieth a ship or a horseman a horse. Then said he, "We need no man's friendship, nor no help of thine. I have heard tell of thee. Thou art not yet grown to man's estate. What can'st thou do?"

"I have harried two summers eastaway," answered

63

Styrbiorn. "And afore that, I slew mine uncle's outlaw, Lambi the White, that was a sea-king of great
note. That was off Skaney-side last summer."

Palnatoki asked whence they were come now.

He answered, "From guesting east in Holmgarth.
And we harried summer-long in Biarmaland and
Balagarth-Side. And not bootless came we thence."

"If hence thou sailest, I think thou'lt leave that booty
here," said Bui.

Sigvaldi spake: "The ships be manned, Toki.
'Twere well an we rowed out forthright: take these
conies, ere they take fright and up scut and away."

Earl Wolf, that was by Styrbiorn on the poop, spake
in his ear: "This is a rash folly, as I told thee. Seest
not how they do lay their noses together in deliberation
what to do? And 'tis not for our comfort nor furtherance."

"Let be," said Styrbiorn. And he called out on high
to Palnatoki, "Take to us: you shall not find that in
seeking friends you found table-guts to eat you and
your meat. And you lack a man, I am for you."

"Thou art a boy," shouted Palnatoki then. "Come
back in a year or twain, with a beard grown. Then
I'll talk to thee." But for all his scornful words, he
stood looking still on Styrbiorn long and narrowly, as
if taken by somewhat in the face of him, or in the carriage and gait of him, or in the voice of his speech.
Styrbiorn's brow blackened at his words.

Bui let out a great laugh, and cried aloud and said,

"Home with thee to thy mammy, crow-chick. If I
have not more hair of my tail than thou of thy face,
let me end my days in a stinking swine-sty as dry-nurse
to the new-weaned yelts."

"There be hand-smiters here as well as tongue-
smiters," said Styrbiorn.

"And I have a switch," cried Bui, "for to smite thy
backside withal."

Palnatoki abode yet looking on him from the wall,
above the lazy wash and lap of the sea-swell. And now
he shouted again to him on the ship and said, "I have
told thee I am no lover of guests nor guestings. But
my redes are reckoned wholesome. And this is my
rede to thee, to put up your helm and get you away from
Jomsburg whiles ye may."

For answer, Styrbiorn let wear his ship yet closer
for easier speech with them on the wall. And now
might they have yet clearer sight of him, and of the
great growth and strength that was his and the fair
and likely seeming of the man, the while he spake
with Palnatoki. And this was the end of their talking, that Styrbiorn said he was not minded to turn away
from Jomsburg, but if they thought him over young
to be had into their law and fellowship, then let them
try it out, since by handy-stripes at equal odds is a man
best known. And for that, let them row out a long-
ship against his with an even number of men to match
those that were with him ashipboard: "And do thou,
Palnatoki, or whoso amongst you is held for the best

man-at-arms, come with that ship to fight with me and
my ship. And if thou slay me, there is an end, and
my men shall yield up all these chattels and gear that
we have fetched from the East aboard our ships. But
if I overcome thee and slay thee, then may the Jomsburgers with right and justice take me for captain in
thy stead, seeing that I should have shown myself by
that deed to be the better man. And these things shall
first be made fast betwixt us by strong oaths unto Thor,
in whom most of all the Gods I do put my trust. And
if there be any other God in whom you of Jomsburg do
put your trust more than in Thor, then shall your oaths
be unto that God and unto Thor besides." Styrbiorn
made Earl Wolf his foster-father speak all this on his
behalf, since he himself made but a poor hand at
speeches.

Now they of Jomsburg spoke many of them against
this at first; and most of all Sigvaldi, which was by
nature from his youth up crooked of counsel and loved
not direct and open dealings, but was as ready for all
deceits and flim-flams as an oyster for a fresh tide. But
Palnatoki, when all was said, spake among them:
"Either of two things have we here: that this is a young
braggart, or else a wolf-cub after mine own heart.
A true word is that, that 'Upward runs the young man's
path.' And that is another, 'Look for a fall when
the tree is old.' I am not the man I have ever known
myself if a boy shall beat me. But if that were fated,

why then ye were better have him than me. And now
I will fight with Styrbiorn, ship to ship."

Styrbiorn said to Earl Wolf, "I will not have thee
with me in this battle, foster-father. For if ill came
to ill, hard put to it were our Swede-folk then, and
these that followed me from the East, to hold by our
oaths for me, and me battle-slain. But if thou wert
there to bridle their high mettle, that might yet be
done."

"It is wonderful," said the Earl, "that I do love thee
well enough to humour thee even in this."

So now was a ram slain and oaths taken betwixt them
of either side, calling ancient witnesses to hear their
vow: by the southing sun, and by the bright lightning-
stream, and by the rock of Victory-Tyr, and by the ring
of Ulli. And therewith must each man say, "If I do
not according to this oath, then let the ship that saileth
under me sail not, though a fair wind blow; and let
the sword I draw bite not, save when it shall sing about
mine own head. And so let it fare with me as it fareth
with a wolf out in the wild-wood: poor and joyless and
without all meat, save that which is gotten with leaping
on carrion corpses." Right eager was Bui the Thick
to be at this battle, but Palnatoki would have none go
with him save his own ship's company only, the same
which were wont to man his ship when they went to
war. "Thou art more stubborn," said Sigvaldi, "than
a kinked hawser in cold weather. And much thou

temptest the fates of death. Yet thou hast ever had
good luck in thine undertakings, and may be that shall
save thee again." Palnatoki bade Sigvaldi take command while himself was away, and man the ships and
keep them in the harbour; "And see that no man of
you is guilty of any unpeaceful deed unless they shall
first break oath with us."

Now Earl Wolf held his fleet away to the northward, and the Jomsburgers lay in their ships within the
open seagates. But Palnatoki rowed out with his ship
against Styrbiorn's and they lay aboard of one another
and fell to fighting without more ado. But the other
ships of either side abode two bow-shots' distance from
them of either hand. Palnatoki was a man well skilled
with arrow and bow, and three or four men of Styrbiorn's he slew in that manner ere they were come to
handy-strokes. But when they were well grappled ship
to ship, then was there a rattle of iron, and weapon play
of the sharpest. And now the fight waxed grim and
woundsome to men, and they of Palnatoki's following
began to go up upon the ship of Styrbiorn, and many of
the Swede-folk gat their deaths.

There was with Styrbiorn a man named Eystein
the Fox, a Norseman by kin out of Halogaland. He
had fared abroad from Norway because of Earl Hakon,
for he had slain one of the Earl's men. So he fared
east across the Keel, and thence east overseas to Holmgarth. Styrbiorn took to him there in Garthrealm, and
thence had him with him when he made war in the

68

coasts of Biarmaland. He was a man well skilled in
arms, and most of all with the axe, and was a great
manslayer. So now Styrbiorn called Eystein to him in
the fight, and biddeth him go with him and put back the
vikings out of the ship. Now was the weapon-brunt
harder yet than afore as they went forth, and in short
space the Jomsburgers were fain to give back some little
under that onset. And now was Eystein in the act to
have leaped upon Palnatoki's ship; but Palnatoki thrust
at him so hard a thrust with a spear on the boss of his
shield that he leaped not well aboard of the ship, but
his foot landed in air between the two ships' sides and
he came pitching forward across the gunwale of Palnatoki's. And in that nick of time, or ever he might
right himself, Bessi Thorlakson fetched him with an
axe-hammer so mighty a blow on the head that all the
brains were beaten out of it. Men say there was a
blood-feud of old betwixt those two, Eystein and Bessi,
and that Bessi when he smote him cried out these words:
"So knock we the harns out of Foxes."

With that, Palnatoki egged on his men right fiercely,
and himself leaped again aboard of Styrbiorn's ship
and slew a man on this side and on that. And now he
drave at Styrbiorn with his spear, but Styrbiorn set his
shield against the thrust and budged no whit. Oft
said Palnatoki in after-days that never till then, nor
never since, had he known the like strength in a man,
that he should stand so starkly under the onset of his
spear that he budged not an inch aback for all his thrust-

ing. But the Jomsburgers set on now with so fierce an onslaught that no man might withstand them; and it came to this at last, that they cleared Styrbiorn's ship, in such wise that he himself stood on the poop fronting them alone, but all his men were dead or felled.

Palnatoki spake: "That is well seen, Styrbiorn, that you did set us a hard sword-game; and this too, that thou art a mighty man of thine hands, and a man of a high heart and a stubborn. And now I will offer thee this, which methinks thou mayest take with much honour: that you shall all go your ways now in peace, and have with you all your ships and gear."

"I will not take that," answered he. "But let me and thee deal now together in single combat. And let all hang on that."

"There is danger in that for thee," said Palnatoki. "For even if God should give thee that glory, to prevail over me, 'tis likely my many brave lads that be here ashipboard with us would be angry with thee beyond all letting or leashing, and they would have thee slain despite all oaths."

"Then send them back," said Styrbiorn, "aboard of thine own ship. And let them take up with them my men that be hurt and tend their wounds. So let them ungrapple their ship and row apart. And thou and I may then try it out at ease among the dead corpses."

Palnatoki looked at him and said, "Thou art hurt already. The blood drips from under thy shield down from thy left shoulder. Why wilt thou not take mine offer and sail away?"

He answered, "It was not in the bargain."

"It is sore against my liking," said Palnatoki, "to send to hell untimely so good a man as thou art, and but for the game's sake only and thine own pig-headedness. It is in my mind the rather to deliver thee from thine own folly: bid my men bear thee down with their shields, and so save thy life."

Said Styrbiorn, "I will not be took alive. Of that be well assured. If that thou beest a man indeed, do as I bid."

"Well," said Palnatoki, "it is sore against my liking. And think well that I am not the man to spare thee any whit, once the grey silver is aloft betwixt us."

"Make haste," said Styrbiorn, "ere I grow stiff with waiting."

So the Jomsburgers at Palnatoki's command gat them back aboard of their own ship, and had along with them all those of Styrbiorn's shipmates that were yet alive: and not one of those was able for his wounds to stand upon his feet and wield weapon.

Palnatoki and Styrbiorn stood now foot to foot on the poop of Styrbiorn's ship. Styrbiorn said, "Thou shalt strike the first blow."

"None ever made me that offer till now," answered Palnatoki; "and from thee I will no wise take it." Styrbiorn heaved up his sword and aimed at him a great

round-armed swashing stroke, but he caught it slant-
wise on his shield and it glented aside in air off the
shield's boss. Then Palnatoki hewed at him with a
down-stroke on the helm, but the sword did not bite,
but glanced down the helm and smote off from it the
left wing and so crashed onward towards Styrbiorn's
shoulder, but he caught it with his shield and turned it.
"There winged I the hawk," said Palnatoki then.

And now for some while they bandied great blows,
but well they warded them, so that no stroke came well
home and neither was hurt. Yet was Styrbiorn bleed-
ing from his former wound in the left shoulder, and
for all his strength and fierceness he moved somewhat
more heavily as the fight went on, as if his wound
irked him and the loss of blood; and his face waxed
wondrous dark and grim, and his breath began to come
in great pants and snorts. Yet never the lighter fell
his sword. But Palnatoki was light and slender of limb,
yet exceeding strong withal, as if his sinews were bands
of iron; and for all he was now well three-and-forty
winters old, he was with all his war-gear light of foot
as a boy at the ball-play, and leaped in and out like a
cat; until, leaping backward from one of Styrbiorn's
mighty flail-sweeps of his sword, his foot came down in
a slime of half-clotted gore, slid from under him like
a skate on new ice, and landed him flat on his back with
his enemy sprung over him weapon in hand.

Styrbiorn gave backwards a pace and lowered his
sword. His face looked grey now, that was so red, and

he spake through gritted teeth. "Stand thou up, and let us play out the play." He leaned, with his right hand that gripped the sword-hilt, heavily on the ship's gunwale. The timbers quivered under his hand.

Palnatoki leaped lightly to his feet again, and faced him again with sword and shield. Looking with his eagle eyes on Styrbiorn, he said, "It will be better for us to give over now. Wise is he that can read the signs of the Gods."

Styrbiorn said, "Thou art a good man, Palnatoki. I would not do a dastard's deed by thee. But let us play out the play."

Palnatoki let fall his sword with a clatter among the stretchers and came to Styrbiorn with open hand: "Better side by side shall the swords of us two bite, than one against the other."

Styrbiorn, all fordone with weariness and bloodletting, had scarce might to grip hands with him.

By then were the fleets of either part rowed up, and great clamour was there, and much likelihood it seemed of a battle-royal now betwixt them. For Earl Wolf and his folk, when they had seen the ships part and the ship of the Jomsburgers row away, were at a set and knew not what to make of it, and so put their ships in motion, meaning to see closer at hand the ending of this matter. Which when Sigvaldi beheld, he bade all row out of harbour and make ready to set upon them out of hand anon, since it was clear that these Swedes were going about to break truce with them and bewray

Palnatoki. And certain it is, it had been short work
of Earl Wolf and Styrbiorn's host had they foughten
it out there against the men of Jomsburg.

But Palnatoki standing high on the poop of Styrbiorn's
ship there, his hand in Styrbiorn's, shouted to them of
both sides with his voice that was like a trumpet of brass,
clear thundering through the hubbub of voices and
clanking oars and waves awash and gurgling, letting
them know the fight was done, and peace given to Styrbiorn. So they harkened to Palnatoki and obeyed his
word.

Now they rowed back, and looked to their wounds,
and Palnatoki leeched them that were badly hurt, for
he was skilled in leechcraft as in many a matter beside.
But the slain they brought ashore in the ships and laid
them in howe by the sea-shore a little east of Jomsburg.
But Styrbiorn and well an hundred of his men that
were of right age and the likeliest among them, these
they took into Jomsburg to be vikings of Jomsburg from
that day forth. Men say that never before was any
man had into Jomsburg that was less than eighteen
winters old, nor, after Styrbiorn, was any man else
had in by them under age save only Vagn Akison alone.
But Palnatoki took to Styrbiorn after their fight together, for he said that never such a man-at-arms had
he known in all his life aforetime, and he said that
there should be no counting of age for such a champion
as Styrbiorn had shown himself to be. And dear
friendship grew up between Palnatoki and Styrbiorn,

74

and there was good liking and friendship between Styrbiorn and all those lords of Jomsburg. Styrbiorn was
with them in their harrying now until winter, and gat
renown, and that winter he sat with Palnatoki in Fion.

Now that same year in Upsala, at winter's end,
Queen Sigrid bare a son to Eric the King.

V

Yule in Denmark

NOW was another year come and gone, and the third winter come of Styrbiorn's being abroad. He was held now for so great a man of war amongst them, and for so wise and foresighted a man for all his youth and his sometimes heat and rashness, and withal he was so well loved of every man of them, that none thought it ill that Styrbiorn should be called captain in Jomsburg whensoever Palnatoki was away out of the burg about his own affairs whether in Fion or otherwise.

There was in those days in Jomsburg Biorn Asbrandson of Coombe, a man of Iceland that was come to Jomsburg a little afore Styrbiorn himself came thither. Biorn was now in the twenty-ninth year of his age, and this by-name he had that men called him Biorn the Broadwickers' Champion. Of most goodly countenance he was, and pleasant of speech, and (by the talk of folk) as big a champion in wooing of women as in holding of his own against men; in both which games there were few might match him. There was good liking betwixt him and Styrbiorn, well nigh from that day when Styrbiorn was first taken into Jomsburg; and now Styrbiorn had bounden Biorn to him with oaths of brotherhood, and had they been brothers born there could scarce closer love and friendship have been betwixt them.

It was the wont of those lords of Jomsburg, when

all the booty was brought home at summer's end and
safely bestowed, to go every one to his own place, leaving force to hold the burg through winter. Only one
of their chiefest men must bide there as captain in
Jomsburg the winter through. They determined by
lot year by year who should have that duty, nor was
any eager to have it, but they took it turn and turn
about. This year was the lot fallen on Heming, the
second son of Strut-Harald the Earl, to be captain in
Jomsburg and abide there until the spring of the year,
when they should all gather thither again against their
summer harryings.

And now were the more part of them ready for their
homeward faring, but Styrbiorn yet debated whither
he should go, for it was not till spring should be well
begun that his due time should come when he might
come home again to Sweden and take up kingdom there,
according to the word of Eric the King.

Now many would have had Styrbiorn go home with
them and spend Yule-tide as their guest, in so much
that there was like to be very mischief amongst them out
of argument which of them should have him. Until
in the end, Biorn said in his ear, "There is good guesting, Styrbiorn, with King Harald Gormson in Denmark.
For thither fared I when first I came east out of Iceland, and King Harald was good to me and welcomed
me well. There is this too, that he hath a daughter
young and meet for wedlock. And this thou hast told
me many a time, that thou was minded to take a wife,

so as thou shouldst be not an heirless man when thou
shalt be set in kingdom in Upsala."

Styrbiorn laughed. Taking Biorn by the arm, he
spake and said among them, "Here be we two, foster-
lings unfostered for the while. Were it not just if the
Dane-King should foster me and thee, Biorn, this Yule-
tide, sith Palnatoki fostereth his brat?"

So those two with their following, when they had
bid farewell to Palnatoki and the rest, sailed west along
the land and so up into the Dane-realm, and there asked
tidings and found that King Harald sat that winter in
Sealand in his great house at Roiskeld. So they sailed
to Sealand and up the firth into the land till they were
come to the head of the firth where it opens as it were
into a great mere or inland sea. As soon as King
Harald heard that the Jomsburgers were come thither,
he sent messengers to bring them greetings and bid
them come to him in his hall which stood up not far
from the sea-side on a little eminence overlooking the
gray land and the gray sea. So they came, and greeted
well the King, and he gave them good welcome, and
bade them be with him over Yule-tide.

King Harald was a man of the greatest largesse,
and he set good fare before his guests and good drink
and of the strongest. That night, ere they went to bed,
were all the Dane-folk swine-drunken, so that they lay
where they slid and snouked and snored till morning;
but Styrbiorn and his folk kept their wits, albeit not a
man of them but drank cup and cup against the Danes.

And King Harald outdrank his folk, yet was overcome at length with his quaffings and lay drunk in his
chair. He was burly of build and quack-bellied and
thick and short of neck and with great chuff cheeks, and
his mouth was ugly, and a monstrous dead tooth lay out
of it over his lip of one side, that had been there these
many years; and it was thence came that by-name by
which men called him through all the Northlands, of
Harald Blue-tooth. Many a night the while they
guested with King Harald he made them the like
good cheer, and always it ended in the same way,
that the Jomsburgers showed themselves the sturdier
drinkers.

Now it was King Harald's wont that every night
when they were set at meat, ere they fell to, the King
let hallow the board by a priest of his that went in a
long-coloured gown like as women use to wear, and
had the top of his head shaven bald and smooth. And
the King had a house nigh to his own house that he
called his kirk, and here must this priest say his mass
at proper seasons, and the King went to mass and all
his folk. But the Jomsburgers went not so. Styrbiorn asked Biorn how came it about that the Dane-
King and his folk would not do worship and trowed no
more in the Gods. "So it is said," answered he, "that
in years gone by Keisar Otto came up against the Dane-
work and bade the Danes take christening. King
Harald said nay to that and all his folk, and held the

82

Dane-work against the Keisar and there was long war
betwixt them. The King sent for Earl Hakon out of
Norway, and the Earl came to help him. But in the
end the Keisar won the Dane-work, and let do christen
the King willy-nilly, him and all his men. And thereafter the King and the Keisar let christen the Earl too,
and his men. But as soon as Earl Hakon was gotten
with his ships out of the land, men say that he went
ashore on an isle that is there and made blood-offering
unto the Gods and so went again ashipboard and so home
to Hladir. And ruleth Norway from that day forth
as he were very King, and never no more payeth no
scat, and counteth not a flea's worth neither christen-
faith nor the King of the Danes, whose Earl he was
aforetime."

"That was well done," said Styrbiorn.

Styrbiorn and his folk were there with King Harald
Gormson in Roiskeld all winter till Yule. There was
not a man of the King's men could stand with Styrbiorn
in feats of strength and skill, nor durst any quarrel with
him nor cross him. At first the King wished to have
him to be his man, and offered him both goods and
land thereto and an Earl's name, if he would leave
Jomsburg and come to him, but Styrbiorn would not.
The King bade him take christening, but Styrbiorn
would have naught of that. And now their friendship,
which had begun hopefully, seemed to grow no more,
but bide where it was, like a thorn set in poor soil on

a windy headland. But with the lads and young men
that were with King Harald that winter in Roiskeld
Styrbiorn was so blithe and gamesome that they loved
him well, and it was easy to see that they took joy to
follow him and back him, and what thing soever seemed
good to him that thing they praised and cried down the
thing that he misliked or cared not for. King Harald,
seeing and considering these things, now began to change
his mind into another tune, and became exceeding glum
when Styrbiorn was by, and short-spoken. Styrbiorn
thought it good game to jest with the King when he was
in a dump and make sport with him. And he would
say now and then to the King in his sport that he knew
not for sure if Harald were a good King for the Dane-
folk, what with his kirk and his priest, and he would
say he was minded sometimes to put some other king
there in Harald's stead and send him packing. King
Harald made as if to take these jests in good part, giving him back flyting answers and making game of it.
But within himself these things rankled, and that more
and more as time went by.

King Harald had but one son, Svein, that was now
at fostering with Palnatoki as is aforesaid. Svein was
as now nine winters old. Thyri was King Harald's
daughter. She was now fourteen winters old, of few
words but with a merry eye. Her hair was black and
of a dainty curling growth, her mouth sweetly shaped
but somewhat large. Folk found it hard to say if she
were exceeding fair to look on or not fair at all, for

84

she seemed both the one and the other by turns. She was not tall of stature, yet of a sweet and noble carriage.

Oft would Styrbiorn and Thyri be a-talking together. Biorn marked how those two, that were wont to be short of speech with other folk, were between themselves full of all talk and merriment; and their talk was easy, as if each knew easily the other's mind, as a man knows the country-side he was bred up in and finds all things there of kin with him. So it went for a time. And now Thyri seemed silenter of speech again, and it was as if the morning freshness of her mood became shadowed a little. Biorn, marking these things, asked Styrbiorn on a day if it were not his mind to open this matter with King Harald, "Sith thou art minded to take a wife; and I can see things sail for thee here both with wind and tide."

"There is time enough yet," said Styrbiorn.

"I had thought, to look on thee, that thy mind was set," said Biorn.

Styrbiorn said, "For friends, that is one thing. But for a wife, I know not."

"But thou lookest for a wife?" said Biorn. "And here to thy hand is a maid the fairest that may be, and like-minded with thee, and of as mighty kindred as thou couldest desire."

Styrbiorn laughed. "May be I like not black women. Or may be I like not little women. And yet I like her. And yet, I will not."

85

So now Biorn let that sleep, and left talking of these things.

Now was Yule-tide come, and King Harald had a great bidding of his mighty men up and down the land to come and keep festival with him, and let sing mass in his kirk. And again he would have had Styrbiorn and his folk take christening, but none of them were minded thereto and the King could not get his way. At night was the King's great Yule-drinking holden. There was much tale-telling there and man-matching.

The King asked Biorn to tell him somewhat about Iceland. Biorn told him.

"Is there no kings in that land?" asked King Harald.

"Not one," said Biorn.

"Then who ruleth there?"

"The priests," said Biorn.

"What, such as this one?" asked the King, pointing with his finger.

Biorn fell a-laughing. "Not so, Lord. Rather, such as I," he said.

"Wast thou a priest then in Iceland, Biorn?" asked the King.

"Nay," said Biorn.

"Why wast thou not a priest?" asked the King.

" 'Tis not for every man," answered he, "to hold that greatness. In my country-side, where I was born and waxed to manhood, was Snorri Thorgrimson priest in my time; and he had the priesthood from his father

86

before him, Thorgrim the Priest of Frey, and it was in their kin and line since the time of Thorolf Most-beard that came first of them out to Iceland and took land at Thorsness."

"Your priests are very like kings?" said King Harald.

"They have much the power of kings," said Biorn, "save that no man need follow and obey them but of his own free choice. And they have not the name of a king nor the state of a king."

"What wast thou in Iceland, Biorn," asked the King, "since thou wast not a priest?"

"I was mine own man," answered he.

"And what couldst thou do?" asked the King.

"I was a pretty man with mine hands," said Biorn.

"Thou wast a pretty fighter?"

"Somewhat of that," said he.

"I have heard tell," said the King, "that there be good skalds in Iceland. What hast thou to say to that, Biorn?"

"There shall never be better skalds found than in Iceland," answered Biorn, "though dale meet knoll."

"Ha!" said the King, "I think thou must be a skald, Biorn. And that would please me more than aught else, if thou wouldst sing a stave or speak forth some ditty or song of thine."

"I have made a drapa on you, King," said Biorn, "of twenty stanzas long. If you will give me leave I will say it forth."

"That pleaseth me well," said the King.

So Biorn stood forth and spake his drapa that he had made in praise of Harald the King, and when it was done all thought Biorn was as good a skald as had been known in the Dane-realm these many years as far back as men might remember. And King Harald was pleased with Biorn's song, and gave him a gold ring weighed twelve ounces.

The King asked Biorn if he knew more songs. Biorn answered and said he had store of songs of many kinds. The King bade him choose whichsoever of his songs he had liefest give them.

Styrbiorn said to Biorn apart, "This is somewhat unholy, this Yule-drinking, with neither blood-sacrifice nor praise of the Gods. Canst thou not speak somewhat in praise of the Gods, Biorn, so that they be not angry with us? and shame these Danes which regard 'em not?"

"I will do that willingly," answered he. "And the willinger, because 'tis thou that askest it."

So now stood forth Biorn a second time before Harald the King. Biorn was pleasant to look on, a big man and a strong, with fair and open countenance and crisp curling hair clipped short to the head and a short beard curly like sheep's wool and growing tight and close. Thralls had piled fuel fresh on the fires, and the tongues of fire licked upward, and the reek hung about the black roof-beams and the lofty pillars of the hall; and the faces of men were red with ale and feasting and the fires' heat and glare, and the bright light of the fires sparkled back from their eyes and from their rings and collars of gold and from the weapons that hung behind them down the long hall's wainscotting of either hand. And this was the beginning of the lay that Biorn the Broadwickers' Champion spake in King Harald's hall: not his own, but the old holy Spae-Wife's Lay which telleth of the beginning of all that is, foretelling also the end thereof, and the ways of the Gods with men.——

Hearing I crave of all Holy Beings,
Of high and low, Heimdall's children.
Wilt thou, Father of the Slain, that forth I tell thee
Outworn things, the oldest I mind me of old?
Of Giants I mind me, gender'd of yore,
Of them which in far days foster'd and fed me.
Nine worlds I mind me of: nine first Mothers:
And a mighty Judge under the mould below.
In the beginning, of yore, Nothing was:
Nor sand there was nor sea nor the surges cold:
Earth was not at all, neither upper Heaven:
Only a Gap was there Gaping: of grass not any.
Or ever the sons of Bor bare up the land,
They that did mighty Middle-earth fashion,
The Sun shone out of the south on the dwelling-stones;
Then was the ground grown with green leafage.
The Sun wheel'd from the south with her brother Moon,
And cast her right hand athwart heaven's border:
The Sun wist not where her seat should be:
The Moon wist not where his main should be:
The Stars wist not where their stead must be.

89

Stone still sat every man of them while Biorn spake the Spae-Wife's Lay. Only as the song went on men seemed to draw nearer together with a gradual motion not to be seen (as hard it is to see the moving onward of stars), as though there were in that song something houseless, that made them huggle together for warmth and light and right flesh and blood. And it was as if the murk and sable night huddled and stirred on the smoky confines of the fire-light behind and round and above the feasters; as if in the murk of it were a myriad watchers, unbeholden yet close, waiting and watching, while Biorn stood forth in the brightness and spoke his Lay. Harald the King sat back in his high seat hunched up in his beard. With one great hairy fist before him on the table he grasped the drinking horn, stock still. His eyes were cast down for the first while; then he raised them and fixed a dark and troubled stare on Styrbiorn, that was set over against the King in the high seat on the lower bench. But Styrbiorn, sitting erect there, seemed to be thinking of nought but of the song. His two hands grasped the pillars of the high seat a little above his head on either side; the polished links of his ring-byrny glinted and slept with his mighty chest's quiet rise and fall; his nostrils widened, as if in the surging wash and rhythm of the great Lay he heard the sea surge beneath his keel, his surf-deer, sweeping him on to where surf and cliff break together on some unimagined shore.

And now was Biorn come to that part of the song
that speaketh of the fostering of that Wolf who—

> Feedeth on the lives of fey men death-doom'd,
> He redeemeth the Gods' heaven red with gore.
> Dark is on the sunshine: no summer after:
> All weathers ill weathers.—*Wist ye yet, or what?*

And now he sang of the latter things: of Ragnarok
and the Twilight of the Gods—

Sate on the howe there and strake harp-string
The Grim Wife's herdsman, glad Eggthér.
Crow'd mid the cocks in Cackle-spinney
A fair-red cock who Fialar hight.
Crowed in Asgarth Comb-o'-Gold,
Fighters to wake for the Father of Hosts.
But another croweth to Earth from under:
A soot-red cock from the courts of Hell.—
　Garm bayeth ghastful at Gnipa's cave:
　The fast must be loos'd and the Wolf fare free.
Things forgot know I, yea, and far things to come:
The Twilight of the Gods; the grave of Them that con-
　quer'd.
Brother shall fight with brother, and to bane be turned:
Sisters' offspring shall spill the bands of kin.
Hard 'tis with the world: of whoredom mickle:
An axe age, a sword age: shields shall be cloven;
A wind age, a wolf age, ere the world's age founder.
Mimir's children are astir, the Judge up standeth,

91

Even with the roar of the Horn of Roaring.
High bloweth Heimdall: the Horn is aloft;
And Odin muttereth with Mimir's head.
Shuddereth Yggdrasill's Ash on high,
The old Tree groaneth, and the Titans are unchain'd—
    Garm bayeth ghastful at Gnipa's cave:
    The fast must be loos'd and the Wolf fare free.
What aileth the Æsir?   What aileth the Elves?
Thundereth all Jotunheim: the Æsir go to Thing.
The Dwarf-kind wail afore their doors of stone,
The rock-walls' warders.—*Wist ye yet, or what?*
Hrym driveth from the east, holdeth shield on high.
Jormungand twisteth in Titan fury.
The Worm heaveth up the seas: screameth the Eagle:
Slitteth corpses Neb-pale: Nail-fare saileth.
A Keel fareth from the west: come must Muspell's
Legions aboard of her, and Loki steereth.
Fare the evil wights with the Wolf all;
Amidst them is Byleist's brother in their faring,
Surt from the south cometh, switch-bane in hand;
Blazeth the sun from the sword of the Death-God:
The granite cliffs clash, and the great gulfs sunder;
The Hell-dead walk the way of Hell, and the Heavens are
      riven—
    Garm bayeth ghastful at Gnipa's cave:
    The fast must be loos'd and the Wolf fare free.

For a minute after Biorn had ended there was dead
quiet. Then that priest leapt up, proffering from his
lips, higgledy-piggledy like water guggling out of a
bottle-neck, all manner of foul speech and blasphemy;

out of which this much was apparent, that he would have the Danes do some mischief to Biorn.   Till in the end one of the King's men that was set beside the priest stood up and laid hold of him, strongly yet not to hurt him, and put him forth of the door.   But the rest sat silent all, shame-faced, ill at ease, and after a little fell a-drinking again, yet with little jollity.   But the King, with his great flat face corpse-livid even in the friendly fire-light, gazed yet on Styrbiorn as if he beheld in him the very presence of Surt with flaming Sword, captaining the fiends in their onset on Valhalla.

VI

The Dane-King's Daughter

THE next day came Thyri the King's daughter to Biorn and took him apart. "Why didst thou speak that bad song before the King yester-night?" said she.

Biorn, that had naught to say, held his peace.

"I know not what was there save thy song," said she; "but the King my father was put in a mighty taking and hath slept not a wink the whole night through."

"I am sorry to hear it," said Biorn. "Yet 'tis oftener that which goeth in at the mouth hath such-like force, not songs, which goeth in at the ear."

"I cannot speak to thee," said Thyri, "if thou wilt laugh."

Biorn said, "I laugh no more, King's daughter." Thyri looked at him with her large eyes, a strange and shy look. She seemed ill at ease. Biorn thought he could see that she was come to him as to a friend in need, and that this silence of hers was part in doubt whether he were a man to trust, and part for the difficulty of the thing, to speak out her mind and thought to another. "And if I did amiss last night," he said, "that would please me best if I might serve you now howsoever I may, to pay for that."

"Well, it is true," said she at last, "that thou canst do somewhat if thou wilt."

She fell silent again. Biorn said, to help her, "I can keep counsel."

97

"Yes, that first," she said. "Most of all, thou must not tell Styrbiorn. I think thou art his friend?" And she blushed red.

"Not friend only, but very foster-brother," answered he.

"And thou must not let him know aught of this," said Thyri, "not with word nor look."

"I can keep counsel," said Biorn. "And I will do your bidding."

"This it is then," said she: "you were best all get you out of the Dane-realm at your speediest."

Biorn heard this with some wonder. "What good is there in that?" said he.

"Wilt thou do it?"

"I have promised you," said Biorn. "But herein hath Styrbiorn the say, and not I."

Thyri said, "Thou art his friend. Thou canst persuade him."

"What reason must I give him?" said Biorn.

Thyri looked at him as if he should find a reason. When he did not, she said, "I have heard tell of folk, when they have had unwelcome guests, have given them such medicines as did soon make a hand of them."

"That reason," said he, smiling, "will not move Styrbiorn."

She said, "Is he hard to move?"

Biorn said, "Hard indeed, if so be he will stand."

Thyri played awhile with the tassel of her gown. She looked up at him, and then away. "I will speak plain to thee," she said. "I'll give thee reason, and thou hast promised me thou wilt not give it to Styrbiorn. The King my father thinketh there is somewhat between me and Styrbiorn. 'Tis foolish, but I have marked him, and I know. There's danger in it. He would not have it so: he hath other plans: King Burisleif."

She looked up swiftly at Biorn, her face dark with blushes. "What?" said he: "the Wend-king? Why, 'tis an old man."

"Not old," said Thyri.

"Enough to father you," said Biorn.

"It is not this we are to talk on," said Thyri. "The King my father loveth me. He loveth not you Jomsburgers."

"Wherefore gave he then his son to Palnatoki to foster?" said Biorn.

"I tell thee he loveth them not," said she. "We Danes love them not. Kings have reasons for doing this and that, or leaving undone. Thou must not ask me: I know nought, save that so it is: and I would have you all be gone lest some ill come of it."

Biorn looked at her for a minute without speaking. Then he said, "You have honoured me to tell me much. Will you be angry with me if I say my mind?"

"No, that would not be fair," said she softly.

"Then," said Biorn, "be not too hasty. True is that, that 'The seaward reefs are washed with the waves.' Time is of our side."

99

For a full minute's space she abode silent, as if weighing his words and her thoughts. "No," she said at length. "Remember, Biorn, thou hast promised me."

Biorn saw well enough that there was no turning her from this. He said, I will do my best. I will draw him away, if so it may be, whether to Skaney or to Fion or Jomsburg or otherwhere. For to Sweden until summer be come he is bound not to go; so we must tarry otherwhere an half year yet, till time is for him to go north to Sweden."

At that word spoken Thyri blanched to the lips. Biorn thought she was on point to fall, and put out his hands to hold her. She reeled back and leant against the wall, and "North!" she said, "Is it North to Sweden? Let him not go. Not North. Not North, Biorn." Biorn thought she was on a sudden out of her wits. She saw his thought on the face of him.

"I will tell thee," she said. "I had forgot it clean all, as if it had not been. But thy saying of North woke it all back again, as if 'twere to dream it anew. It was a dream I dreamed last night. And methought I was in my father's hall, and the lights burning, and you lords of Jomsburg here in great company. And methought Styrbiorn was waxen so huge of growth, the hand of him was like a platter, and the head of him smote the roof-beams. And methought he lifted up an horn full of mead and cried out with a great voice, crying and saying:

'North 'tis, and North 'tis, and ne'er may we linger!'

"Then methought he laid hold on the King my father with his great platter hand, and had him forth of the hall into the night, and it seemed rain and sleet; and every man that was there ran out, following Styrbiorn and obeying him, and they ran their ships down to the sea, and sailed North with a great wind. After that, it seemed to me in my dream that there were women riding in the sky betwixt lightning and lightning, helmed and byrnied, and terrible was the clang of their bowstrings. And I looked and it was as if the ground was thick with the dead bodies of men battle-slain, and ravens and wolves were gathered thither under the darkness to feast on the dead bodies. Then in my dream I began to look upon the faces of the slain. And I looked and saw him too, lying there slain. And then it was as if the night ebbed backward from me on every side, like the sucking back-wash of the sea, and it was pitch dark, And I woke not, but must have fallen on deep sleep out of my dream, and so waking at day-break remembered nought. Only thy saying North brought it back to me."

She paused, and stood panting, looking at Biorn as if for help, her hand pressed hard against her bosom.

"There be dreams and dreams," said Biorn gently. "There is but one way for a man, and that is to remember that none may avoid his fate. This is to a man as the due ballast to the ship, which maketh the vessel indeed loom somewhat deeper, but keepeth it from tossing too lightly upon the uncertain waters."

"Work for me in this," said Thyri, as if she had

marked nought of what he said. "Take him away hence. Keep him out of Sweden, for all sakes. Thou must not by word or look bring me into it. Thou must swear to me."

Biorn took her hand in his. "I will swear that," he said.

In that same while was Harald the King walking back and forth with Styrbiorn before the King's garth. And all the time was the King a-talking, and his talk came ever and again to the same point and shied away from it, like a bad horse whose rider putteth him again and again at a jump and he refuseth again and again. But this was plainly the King's mind, whereas he had but a month since been ever desiring that Styrbiorn should bide there in Denmark and be his man, naught would serve his turn now but to be quit of Styrbiorn and rid him out of the land. And ever as they walked and talked Styrbiorn bethought him of that look in the King's eyes the night before when the King had looked on him at the ending of Biorn's song. And he knew in his bones that it was the look of a man that seeth and knoweth his master, and feareth him and hateth him for his mastery and hateth his own little strength. So while King Harold talked and beat about the bush, Styrbiorn pleased himself with the memory of that caged-bear look of last night: and there ran pleasure sweetly within him with a secret caress of every member of his body, as of old when he pinned down Moldi by the horns and

tasted power and dominion, but sweeter now and more
dangerous, feeling under his hand the great King of the
Danes 'stead of a brute beast.

And after a while he was ware of the King saying to
him how it were fitter he should go forthright home to
Sweden and claim his own, rather than sit a-guesting in
foreign lands, howsoever welcome a guest; and how men
should deem him but soft and little-hearted and a man
of little account, if but at one man's bidding he should
go meekly away and stop away as long time as he was bid.
That was a likelier way to show the King his uncle what
mettle he was of, to tarry no more, but come home now
with that force of men and ships to back him and claim
his right now, in his own time not another's.

Now such counsel as this, coming from the King upon
Styrbiorn in his secret lust-fired mood of power, had
like swift and unlooked-for effect as if a child should
throw a cup of water into a pan of molten metal. He
swung him about so sudden fierce that the King, for all
his unwieldly weight of guts, leapt a pace back and away
from him as light as a startled doe, and clapped hand
to sword-hilt. Spite of his anger and rage Styrbiorn
brake out a-laughing. Then he said in his swift stuttering way, "in many lands have I guested but never, till
now, found I lords or kings so niggardly nor so shame-
less as chase guests away and grudge 'em their entertainment. May be 'tis your worshipping of dirty gods hath
learned you these ways."

"These be shameful words," said the King: "I

never bade thee go but for thine own good. But now I
see thou art worse to deal with than I had thought for."

"When I come again," said Styrbiorn, "I will show
thee and thy Danes if I be a man slow to take mine own
or not."

With that, he let call up his folk and bade them pack
up the stuff and launch the ships, because forth of the
Dane-realm he was minded to depart that very hour.
They thought this a strange wild turn, and muttered and
grumbled long enough, yet went about it briskly enough
for all that. For so strangely was he in not two years
grown into the hearts of them, of well nigh every man
that was in Jomsburg, that naught seemed too hard or
too useless or too much against their liking, but at his bidding they would do it without question, deeming not life
itself too dear a thing to spend in his service.

And so it was that Biorn, coming forth with Thyri's
bidding on his hand, found the work done for him ere he
made his first step towards it. When by questioning of
Styrbiorn he had gotten the truth of the matter, he said,
"That were ill, if we should part now unfriends with
King Harald Gormson. And this is my counsel, that
Bessi Thorlakson and I should go to the King and speak
good words to him and that you be set at one before we
sail away."

"Do as thou wilt," said Styrbiorn. "But I will not
make myself little before him."

"It is not good," said Bessi, "that there should be ill

104

blood betwixt us of Jomsburg and the Dane-king."

Styrbiorn said, " 'Tis small matter one way or 'tother. He knoweth we Jomsburgers be the better men, and able to rule him and we would."

"Well if he know it," said Bessi. "But it would try his temper over much if we should let him see we know he knoweth it. That is where thou hast dangered us."

Styrbiorn laughed and shook his head: "Thou talkest as good riddles as doth old Thorgnyr, that the King mine uncle holdeth in so great account in Sweden. I never could make head nor tail of 'em."

The end of it was that Biorn and Bessi did their errand so well that all was made smooth again betwixt King Harald and Styrbiorn. When they bade the King farewell he said, "This maketh great wonder to my mind, Styrbiorn, that thou shouldst choose to put to sea in mid-winter and of an evil stormy day to boot. And yet a greater wonder that they will follow thee in this." Styrbiorn said nothing, having promised not to bandy words with the King. The King gave Styrbiorn gifts at parting, a helm and a sax-knife with haft of gold. Styrbiorn gave the King a Greek hat and a silver baldrick set with amber.

So they came down to the shore of the sea and went ashipboard. The lift was all overspread with dirty cloud, and there were gray stacks of storm-cloud piled far away on the bourne of the sky to seaward. The sea was dark like iron, flecked with white horses, and with a livid band of light in the far distance. There was a biting wind blew from the north-east.

"Wither shall we sail now?" asked Biorn, "if we be not to be drowned?"

Styrbiorn answered and said, "We will sail North."

VII

Eric and Styrbiorn

THE King had with him in Upsala in those days three men whom he held in good esteem. They were not good friends with the throng of people, and many thought it as near a bit to call them ill-doers as call them men of valour. They were named Helgi and Thorgisl and Thorir. None knew the father or kindred of any one of them, but most folk thought they must be King Eric's bastards, and that for this sake his eye rested kindly on them. For this was much noted of the King as his years wore, no less then aforetime, that he was mightily given to women, and kept not to his own.

These three on a day walked up and down a-talking together and making game, when there passed by before them without the King's hall Sigrid the Queen. She was whiter than a sunbeam on a bright day; and she carried the child of her and Eric, that was named Olaf, in her arms. And the child was now about a twelve-month old.

Thorgisl said, "There goeth one shall be King yet in our time."

"That is to be looked for," said Helgi; "unless Styr-biorn send him first to a cold lodging. For, 'a foe's child is a wolf to cherish.'"

"For men of our mettle," said Thorir, "a lap-king were a better choice then Styrbiorn, when he cometh home."

"A lap-king? What is that?" said they.

"One that should sit quiet in his mother's lap," said Thorir, "and leave us to follow our sport."

Helgi said, "I know not how it seemeth to you two, but to me it was ever a wonder that Styrbiorn bestrode not this mare, and the foal were not his rather than the King's. I have smelt matters betwixt them now and then."

"How? Is not princesses in Holmgarth enough for him?" said Thorir.

But Thorgisl said, "I never found thy tongue too slow, Helgi. Thou wert better let alone that bad talk."

"Have it as thou wilt," said Helgi. "Howbeit, I leave you there a fair pool for a dry tongue to fish in. We may turn it to some good use next year, belike, if he come home to play the King here."

"I think," said Thorir, "that we three have had trouble enough, each man of us, with this young quat, should make us unwilling to wear our lives out under his shadow. But we must be mindful of this, that he hath waxed mightily in these two years he hath been abroad out of the land, and will be waxed yet more next year."

So went the talk of those three. But the next news in hand, a day or two after, was no smaller matter than this: that Styrbiorn was come into the Low with an hundred ships. Men wondered much at this and much guessing there was, what the King was like to do, and how he would take this home-coming of Styrbiorn's

months before his due time. And that was in the mind
of most of them, that this was carried with too high a
hand for the King to let it pass; so that they who wished
well to Styrbiorn were sorry when they heard of his
coming, but his ill-willers were glad at heart.

Styrbiorn left the host of his ships in the Low, and
himself rowed with a few ships up to Sigtun and there
took horse and came to find the King his uncle in Upsala. At their meeting was naught asked nor answered
betwixt them openly, how long he was minded to stay
nor what was to be thought of his unlooked-for coming.
Nor was aught said, either by Styrbiorn or by the King,
that might let men know clearly if the King were
minded to punish this disobedience or to swallow it.
The King seemed to bear himself somewhat coldly and
aloof from Styrbiorn; and as days went by, and all
quiet, men knew not what to make of it. Some thought
the King was over kind to Styrbiorn and could not find
it in his heart to put force on him. Some two or three,
that had little wit, thought the King was afeared of
him. Thorgnyr and they that knew the King best
thought they knew that he held his hand of a purpose,
seeing in this thing a trial of Styrbiorn whether he would
yet of his own accord do right at last without stress
nor argument laid on him.

On a day men made a great gathering at the tarn
called Kysingtarn for playing at the ball. Styrbiorn
was there and with him they that were chiefest among
his following: Biorn Asbrandson, namely, the Broad-

wickers' Champion, and Bessi Thorlakson, and Gunnstein Lowry, and Odd o'Marklands, and other men of note among the Jomsburgers. So when folk were now come together to the tarn Styrbiorn went straightway to Helgi, where he stood along with Thorir and Thorgisl, and asked them to play with him.

"That will we gladly," answered they.

"Let us share out the sides for the game," said Styrbiorn. "I and my Jomsburgers shall be of one side to play against you stay-at-homes of the other. That will be the greatest sport."

"We shall like that well," answered Helgi.

"The greatest sport?" said Biorn: "but belike the greatest make-bate. That will be better, Styrbiorn, if thou be of one side, and Helgi of the other side along with me. And the rest you may share out evenly, some of our folk and some of your own countrymen here of either side."

Styrbiorn said he cared not which way it should be, so the game were good.

"That will be better," said Helgi then, "even as Biorn hath counselled. For you of Jomsburg are of such might and prowess in all feats, ye were sure to get the better of us if we were pitted against you: and that the more, Styrbiorn, seeing thou art become so great a man: in every other place I mean, save in Sweden alone, and that thine own native land and rightful realm."

And now they went to share out the sides as Biorn

would have it. In the meantime not once nor twice only but many times would those companions, Helgi and his, be keeking and girding at Styrbiorn to the like tune; and every time he laughed them off in seeming carelessness and merriment, as if he imagined not into what port their rotten bark would arrive.

When they began their game there was not a man might stand up against Styrbiorn, nor bear away the ball if he were in the way. He played most against Helgi, and Helgi gat ever the worst of the market when they two came together. Until on a time when Helgi would have held him to keep him from the ball, Styrbiorn caught him and cast him down so rudely on the hard ice that for a minute's space or more he abode there senseless, and the blood gushed out of his nose, and his knees and knuckles were scraped raw with the rough ice. Helgi thought he saw Styrbiorn's drift now. He liked this handling little enough; but he could not for shame cry out upon it, since it was in the game. And now Biorn of the other side flung the ball so hard at Thorir, taking him fair in the belly, that it knocked all the breath out of his body.

Earl Wolf was there with Thorgnyr the Lawman looking on at the game. He said to Thorgnyr, "It is easily seen which be here the stronger players, though the sides be fairly matched."

"There is envy enough and discontents," said Thorgnyr, "without these plays to blow them bigger."

"Thou and I are not every day set forth on the same

road," said the Earl; "nor, an we were, is it always easy for us to walk together without jostling. But I think we are at one in this, that we would gladly bid farewell to my foster-son until winter's end, according to the King's word and his own."

"Many," said Thorgnyr, "would blithely bid Styrbiorn farewell, but not all would wish him safe return."

"I know not that," said the Earl. Then he said, "Let us two be open with one another. Canst thou guess what is in the King's mind?"

Thorgnyr gave him a look from under his deep-shadowing eyebrows. "I can guess as well as thou canst."

"What say Helgi and his?" asked the Earl. "Methinks thou art in their secrets."

"They are no friends of mine," said Thorgnyr.

"No," said the Earl. "But that sayeth not that they would not gladly use thy wisdom."

"I am not to be used by other men," answered he, "except only by the King. Or is that news to thee?"

"That I knew too," said the Earl then. "And therefore have I wondered somewhat that Helgi and Thorgisl and Thorir should be so oft in thy company. But then I bethought me that, all and if no man is able to use thee for his tool, yet thyself wilt not stick, belike, to use the first tool thou shalt light on, so only thou mayst thereby avail to shape the matter as thou wouldst have it."

The Earl, so speaking, watched him narrowly. But as much might he learn from a carven pillar as from that old man's face. Thorgnyr spake: "He is a man of sense, none can gainsay it, who will make shift with a dung-fork if he lack spear. But why shouldst thou think, for a matter of this kind, I'd need either? I can bide my time."

Now snow began to fall in swirling eddies of large white feathery snow-flakes. Yet they played on as briskly as ever. The Queen looked on at the game, muffled in a cloak of woollen stuff that was dyed the colour of the rowan leaf in the first nip of autumn and lined with swansdown. She had drawn the hood of it up over her ears, so that the proud and lovely face of her and the bright hair above her brow looked out as it were from a doorway or ice-cave mouth of snow-like whiteness; and her face was bright with the snow's touch and the biting air, and her eyes most bright and eager as she followed the game. Folk marked her so standing and watching, and man said to man, "This is a strange new fashion, that women should wish to look on the ball-play, and in this wild weather."

And now thicker and thicker fell the snow, until the ball was hid by it from the players and they from each other. So now they break up the game. The Queen walked beside Styrbiorn as they went back to the King's house: she said, "Thou hast outplayed them all at the ball-play, kinsman Styrbiorn; and that were something to brag of in a bonder's son."

"King's son or carle's son," answered he, "it stirreth the blood."

She looked up at him, and her face was like red dawn on the high snow-fields. "Thou hast outwearied them," she said. "And yet seem'st thyself scarce breathed."

"Wearied!" said he: "not a man of 'em. Not even Helgi." He looked down, met her eyes, and laughed.

When they came to the hall nothing would please the Queen but that Styrbiorn should go with her into her bower, where her tire-women sat at broidering and her nurse with the Queen's young son in her arms. The nurse brought her the child that opened his arms and laughed, but the Queen bade her keep it and bring ale for Styrbiorn. So that was brought in a horn gold-rimmed, and the Queen made Styrbiorn drink and sit down near her beside the fire. There, he looking much in the fire and she on him, they sat a-talking: the Queen saying most, calling to mind old times, asking him of his doings abroad these two years past, of Garth realm and Biarmaland and Wendland and Jomsburg. To all this Styrbiorn answered with but a short word here and there, for never was he a great talker: laughing at whiles, musing in a quiet content, lulled and caressed with the warm sweet accents of her speech that worked subtly in his blood like the luxurious influence of old wine, deep and calm; repose strangely pleasant after violent things: warmth after wind and snow.

Shorter and shorter grew the speech between them,

and the silences longer. After one long silence the Queen, bending down to pick up a brand half-burnt that had tumbled from the fire, said suddenly, "Why art thou come hither again before the time?"

"I could not help it," answered he.

"Why?" she said.

He frowned, then smiled: "I know not. I could not."

"But why didst thou come?"

"I have told thee."

"It was against the King's command," said she.

"He hath said naught against it."

"There was that in Sweden could draw thee—even from Holmgarth?"

He said nothing.

"And yet there be pleasant folk in Holmgarth?"

"Like enough," said he.

"I have heard tell of them. What drew thee hither, then?"

"I know not. Somewhat. This, that I could not help it. Nigh three years abroad: 'twas enough for the while."

Albeit the sun was still some hours from his set, a dim light only it was that came from out of doors from the snow-eddying grey air and sky; but the fire-light shot up from under. And the fire-light gilded with ruddy gold the square proud features of Styrbiorn's face and brow, the massive arms and throat of him, the great and masterful mouth and jaw, all warm in the fire-light's pulsing radiance and beautiful with splendid youth: the down yet soft on his cheek, and the hair of his head strong-curling, short, thick, and coloured like pale mountain-gold.

The Queen spake: "I have watched thee, kinsman Styrbiorn, at the ball-play. That were sport now, and a thing to pleasure me, if I might look upon thee harnessed and weaponed, as thou art wont to go whenas thou leadest out the war-gathering of the vikings of Jom. Let me see thee so."

"I have not my weapons here," said he.

"It is to please my phantasy," said the Queen.

"It is a folly," said Styrbiorn.

"Is it then too great a thing for thee to grant me?" she said. Then, her eye lighting on arms that hung on the big-timbered wall before them: "Why, these will serve."

"What's this?" said Styrbiorn. "The King's mine uncle's?" He stood up from his seat, a little uncertainly, as if this whim of hers carried the jest something beyond the bound of jesting. But she too had risen and would hear no word, crying on her women to lift down the rich-wrought byrny and great eagle-winged helm of Eric the King, and the rimmed shield and the greaves of polished bronze. These last she herself buckled on Styrbiorn's legs, he laughing the while at the whole matter, somewhat shamefacedly, as at some mad prank scarce fit for him to play with, being no longer in his child's age. Yet is it to be thought that he felt it was not wholly child's play: the touch of the Queen's hands gliding with a swift and caressing motion along the great muscle of his calf, as she made fast the fastenings of the greaves. He stepped back as a man might step who has blundered into another's chamber. Not to lose countenance with her, he laughed yet the more boisterously, taking the King's helm that a woman proffered to him and setting it on his head. So that there he stood in the fire-light's splendour, helmed and byrnied and with shield on arm, and girt with the King's sword silver-studded. Erect and grand, as of an eagle alighting from his skyey eminence, the brown wings spread upward from the helm on either side. With lips parted, the Queen looked. She spake no word.

"The gear fitteth me?" said Styrbiorn.

The Queen met his laughing glance with no answering smile. Only under the silken bosom of her gown her breast lifted suddenly like the sudden filling of a sail at sea, and her dark eyes opened on him very wide and tense. She mastered herself on the instant, and was all cool and easy jollity. But to Styrbiorn, who was not yet so young but he had learned to know well enough by this time of day where the little coney loves to scout, that wide-eyed look spoke a language plump and plain.

"What of my young kinsman?" said he. "Wilt sail with me, lad, when thou'rt of age?" And he took the child from the nurse and held it high over his head, dancing it in air. But the child was frighted, and puckered up its face and screamed.

Now it so befell that Helgi was stood in the doorway looking on in this nick of time. He went now to find his friends Thorir and Thorgisl, and they talked together long and low. After that, they went to find Thorgnyr the Lawman. They were somewhat slow in coming to the point with him, but Thorgnyr was pleasant with them and led them on to talk freely. And at length they unlocked to him that which abode in their mind, that it was now the happy hour to pull the bench from under Styrbiorn, and that the means thereto lay ready to hand: namely, to let the King know plainly that it was common talk in the house that Styrbiorn and Sigrid were overgood friends together, and to let him know that Styrbiorn was minded to snatch by force not his own heritage only before his time but the whole kingdom from out of his uncle's hand: "And that he sitteth openly in the Queen's bower, and all as if he were already set in the King's stead, both in bed and hall; and striketh too and spurneth the King's own son, which crieth out and weepeth pitifully."

"Which of you will tell this tale to the King?" asked Thorgnyr.

"This was in our mind," answered Thorir, "that this should be the hopefullest way, if thou wouldst be willing to talk to the King, Thorgnyr: if indeed thou deemest well of our redes."

"When it cometh all to all," said Thorgnyr, "is there a word of truth in the whole story?"

"Say there were not," said Helgi: "'twill come true afore the tale be told."

"Fruit is best gathered when 'tis ripe," said Thorgnyr. "As for this tale of yours, it will not fill half the nostril of a cat. I'll have naught to do with it."

"Come with me," said Helgi then. "I'll show it thee through the chink of the Queen's door."

"No," said Thorgnyr. "I am not a pryer into chinks and look-holes."

So they went out from Thorgnyr very ill content.

"What's to do next?" said Thorgisl.

"What but to go to the King ourselves?" said Helgi.

"He will not heed us," said Thorir.

In the end they were of this mind, that may be it was best for them to say naught of it for the present. "Only we will not cease to flatter and egg him forward to some open violence, which shall give the King just pretext to do him away ere a worse thing befall."

Styrbiorn put off the King's armour and betook him to the great hall. Here he sat quiet till supper time, and spake to no man. Men deemed it strange to see him so quiet and brooding. Before supper he came to the King. "Lord," he said, "I did ill to come back before the time. I will ride down to the ships at daybreak and fare abroad again."

"That is well spoken," said the King, and took him by both hands.

"It was not to vex you I came hither," said Styrbiorn. "It was a long time. It seemed to me I could not help but come. You have been good to me; and now I will go away and keep to the bargain."

They gripped hands and said no more. But there was great content in the King's eyes as they met Styrbiorn's.

The King brought Styrbiorn and his men down to the ships next day. They took leave of both parts with great kindness, and the ships rowed out of the Low and were no more seen. The King rode with Thorgnyr on their way home. Thorgnyr held his peace. After a while the King said, "Thou art a wise man, Thorgnyr, but I think I have taught thee somewhat."

Thorgnyr looked at him awhile in silence. Then he said, "It is not to be denied, King, that you have played well; and you have gotten that you played for."

The King was like a man that hath borne over long time a difficult burden and, casting it down at length where he would have it, breatheth free and seeth all fair before him. He looked at Thorgnyr with a twinkling eye. "It is hard for thee, Thorgnyr, but thou must own thou wast wrong."

"I was not wrong," said Thorgnyr.

"No more," said the King then in a sudden anger. "Thou wast wrong."

But that old man looked sullenly before him, riding northward at the King's side. He said again, under his breath, "I was not wrong."

VIII

The King and the Queen

IT was yet dark winter. Styrbiorn, he and his, sailed south along the land and came, after an ill voyage yet without unhap or loss, to Skaney. Here they put in with their ships and went up to the great house of Strut-Harald the Earl, who gave them noble welcome and kept them with him till winter's end.

Strut-Harald sat in Skaney in those days in state like unto a king, and was a very magnificent man in his house-keeping and had alway guests coming and going. In all Skaney-side his word went as a king's, and there was no man there but held him in the greatest worship and esteem and was ready at all tides to do his bidding. He stood no more now in wars and harryings, being very old and unmeet for fighting. Yet was he no whit the more for that thrust into the corner, as sometimes it befalleth to an old man past his strength, for he had powerful sons and sons-in-law and young men of his blood always under his hand honouring him and upholding his state. And he was a man glorious to look upon even in his deep old age, being nowise bowed down as is the manner of old men, but whether walking or sitting, straight-shouldered and broad-chested and with a proud and high carriage of the head. A big man and a tall he was, great-boned, lean in his old age. He would be clad always in exceeding costly attire, having his garments of rich and lovely colours, and jewelled ornaments of price, and his weapons fairly fashioned and of rare workmanship. And he wore always on his head, within door and without, an hat which was covered with round plates of gold of the bigness of the palm of a woman's hand. So that many there were who thought, when they considered Earl Strut-Harald in his state and wearing that hat which had more gold about it than many a king's crown, that none save only the mightiest kings dwelt in greater circumstance of splendour and magnificence than he.

Sigvaldi and Thorkell the High were there with the Earl their father in Skaney, and had been there all the winter. They were glad at their friends' coming and Styrbiorn's, and the days and weeks went by in good pleasure and contentment until spring.

When Styrbiorn came to Strut-Harald to bid him farewell, the Earl held him a long time by both hands and looked at him long time without word spoken. Then he began to say, "I would thou wert my son. For my sons, good though they be, I deem not good enough. Heming can steer a ship and can make good play with sword and spear, but methinks he will ever have that nature to follow still where another leadeth. Thorkell is a man of war, but he hath little wit. Sigvaldi is a fox. He will get him lordship and wealth and fame and a long life: many men will follow and obey him, but the best men will not praise him. And, true it is, unto few men is it fated to be great, and

126

of fair fame, and long-lived. I think, Styrbiorn, that the first two of these will be thine. But I think thy life will be short."

The Earl's eyes were very blue and keen-glancing. It seemed to Styrbiorn that they rested not on himself when they looked at him, but on some matter afar off, unseen by other men. Styrbiorn said, "I reck not the number of my days, so they be good."

"Fare thee well," said the Earl. "I wish thou wert my son."

From Skaney Styrbiorn sailed first south over the sea to Jomsburg. There sailed with him those sons of Strut-Harald, Sigvaldi namely and Thorkell, with many ships of theirs and a great following, and they abode certain days in Jomsburg. And thither came, some to-day and some to-morrow till they were all gathered thither, the other lords of Jomsburg, Palnatoki and Bui of Borgundholm and Sigurd his brother and many more, until the burg was filled with men and the harbour thick with long-ships, like a stagnant pool under sallows in the season of the year when the leaves do fall, and the leaves of the sallows lie so many on the face of the pool that hard it is to tell whether it be water there or firm land hid with the leaves.

Now they took counsel together, spring being come and the time now ended of Styrbiorn's being abroad. Many were fain to have fared north with Styrbiorn into Sweden to see the King there and to see Styrbiorn received into kingdom. But Styrbiorn said he would not go home thither until summer's end. "How is that?" said they. "Is not thy time come now that summer setteth in, and thou hast been abroad three winters?" He answered, "That may be, but I shall have mine own way in this."

So Styrbiorn sailed a-harrying the fourth summer with Palnatoki and the host of the Jomsburgers. Biorn Asbrandson the Broadwicker's Champion was his shipmate, and men thought they could see how day by day the love and friendship of those two waxed and strengthened. Biorn was with him when he and Bui fared north into Biarmaland and the unknown places of Kirialaland, being thither drawn by the many tales in men's mouths concerning that land: how that in Kirialaland only Finns and skin-changers do inhabit, such as be not alway of one shape nor alway in that same place where they do seem to be; moreover that they of Kirialaland do observe an idol of great note, Jomala by name, that weareth a silver belt about his middle, in a temple in the darkness of a wood that is fulfilled of trolls and evil wights so as a man shall be drove clean out of his wits for very fright sake if he durst adventure there save by favour of Jomala. Styrbiorn and his folk coming to that place found not indeed any troll nor skin-changer, but they sacked Jomala's temple and took the belt of him, that was of a fashion that none yet had seen, wrought with nickers and other worms intertwisted, and took besides so great a spoil of silver and costly treasures as no man could ever remember to have seen taken in one place and in a single day.

Besides Biorn, Styrbiorn had now more than three score men who were his shipmates always and followed him as a picked bodyguard in every warlike enterprise he took in hand. The more part of these had been many years vikings in Jom, as Bessi Thorlakson, Thorolf Attercop, Howard the Hewer, and Alf Braggart: others, as Gunnstein Lowry, were of his first following out of Sweden before he came to Jomsburg: other some he had taken to in many lands, men who had first felt the might of him as their conqueror in battle and were now the closer bound to his love and service, lords and princes of the east, Valdimar, the great Prince's son of Holmgarth; Ere-Skeggi, that was young brother to an earl in Estland; Olaf the Wend, and many more. And like as Palnatoki by the mastery of his mere presence kept peaceable all those overweening men of war as many as followed in those days the Lay of the Jomsburgers, so in his own ship's company Styrbiorn held in comradeship men of far diverse speech and blood, and so proud withal and quarrelsome of nature that, but for him, they had fallen daily like wolves each at another's throat. So Styrbiorn made great warfare eastaway, and fought both by sea and land and subdued many warlike peoples that withstood him long time, but ever in the end Styrbiorn had the victory, and much wealth they took there.

But when it wanted now but five weeks of winter, Styrbiorn busked him for his faring into Sweden. He deemed it not good that he should come home this time with too great a force of ships nor too many men along with him, lest the King his uncle should think that showed unfriendly, as if he, to whom the King had plighted his faith solemnly and obliged himself to grant him kingdom now and his father's heritage, should come in a manner to misuse his favourer and claim it with drawn sword. Howso, there fared with him Bessi Thorlakson and Gunnstein and others of lesser note: ten ships in all. Biorn fared not this time with him into Sweden, but being taken with a sickness abode in Jomsburg. But the more part of the Jomsburgers held the sea still, for it was not their way to leave harrying till winter set in.

Styrbiorn and his men sailed north with a fair wind, and in good time came through the Low and went ashore at Sigtun. And there was Eric the King with a great company ridden down to Sigtun to welcome Styrbiorn. The King, when he saw him come aland, lighted down from his horse and made haste to meet him, and Styrbiorn came striding quickly over the big stones and up the shelving rough ground of the firth's margin, and they gripped hands and stood so a minute, and then the King drew Styrbiorn to him and embraced and kissed him. Styrbiorn had grown and waxed mightily even in these six months since he came before to Sweden, and albeit King Eric overpassed most other men in greatness of growth, yet men marked now that even with the advantage of the ground (for the King stood on the slope and Styrbiorn below him towards the water-side) the King's eyes looked but level with Styrbiorn's, and the limbs of Styrbiorn seemed greater than the King's and his breadth of shoulder broader and his chest deeper. Men that watched them at that meeting said that never had they seen very father and son fainer of one another than those two. And certain it is, there was no child of his own body that King Eric set such store by as he set by Styrbiorn.

So now was all made ready, and the ships drawn up aland, and the gear packed on wains and a-horseback, both their own stuff and many good gifts which Styrbiorn had brought from Jomsburg to give unto the King his uncle, and they took horse and rode all in company northward towards Upsala.

Styrbiorn rode hand by hand with the King. They talked of this and that. Styrbiorn was somewhat silent and ever again let fall their talk, as if there were something he was eager to hear but would not himself speak first of. As they rode on, and the King still spake of this and that but naught of the main matter, Styrbiorn waxed yet the more ill at ease and yet shorter of speech; but he held himself in well. The King, who saw all this very plainly, made no haste to end it. At length, when their journey was three parts done and they rode up over the brow of a little wooded knoll of ground which had the top as it were a table of the native rock bare as a man's hand above the trees, whence they looked north over the vast uplandish country and wood and water and might see, some miles off, the houses and temple at Upsala, the King drew rein and said to him, "Three weeks hence hath a Thing been called whereat thou shalt be taken to King in Sweden, along with me, even as was thy father aforetime."

"Have my thanks for that, Lord," said Styrbiorn, and took the King's hand in his. The King was looking on him, but he on Upsala. And the King marked how the whole port and bearing of him was altered now, and how the face of him, that was clouded, was bright now like the land's face at point of day.

They rode on. After a time the King began to say, "That were good now, Styrbiorn, now that thou art come to man's estate and takest up kingdom, that thou shouldest take a wife. Or what thinkest thou of that?"

Styrbiorn answered, "I have thought on't. And 'tis most needful."

"Doth thine eye rest anywhere that seemeth good to thee for this?" asked the King. "Thou hast fared abroad in many lands these three years, and I never yet heard tell of so bad a land that it bred not a fair woman or twain."

Styrbiorn laughed. "That is true enough, King. Yet I know not. For a wife——"

"'Tis two matters: to have, and to keep?" said the King.

132

"I have found none yet," said Styrbiorn.

"I will tell thee," said the King, "what hath been in my mind. There is King Harald Gormson hath a daughter, Thyri. That were a match many kings would deem them lucky might they get her. The maid is fair, too, as men tell me, and good-mannered, and of fourteen winters old."

Styrbiorn said, "I knew her, when I was there a-guesting last Yule-tide."

"Well?" said the King.

"I like her well. But I had not thought on't," answered Styrbiorn.

"If she should please thee, that should please me well," said King Eric. "But it is for thine own choosing."

Styrbiorn said, "I had not thought on't. But here, as in other things, your rede shall be mine, Lord."

When they were come home to the King's house in Upsala there was great welcoming of Styrbiorn, wherein was none more forward to take him by the hand than Helgi and Thorgisl and Thorir, they saying many times the same thing till he was something weary of it: that there was not a man in the realm of Sweden but was blithe and glad to see Styrbiorn come again into the land and would be fain of him as King and would back him and further him every way they might. Thorgnyr welcomed him with such warmth and eagerness as a curst old ban-dog or mastiff might welcome a stranger withal whom his master will entertain but

himself would gladly grip his teeth in him if none else
were by to hinder it. The Queen greeted him coldlier
than for their old friendliness might have been looked
for. She said little, came little in his company, went
soon away whenever they chanced together, yet would
still be looking on him when she saw her time and
neither he nor any other could observe it.

Oft would the King take Styrbiorn and show him all
that was there, both old and new, and among other
good things the old house of the King his father, King
Olaf's, where he dwelt when he was yet alive and
where Styrbiorn was born; and King Eric had let mend
and dight it within and without, both the main hall and
the chambers thereof, and fit it with new hangings and
all kind of gear: "And this shall be thine own house,
Styrbiorn, to dwell in when thou takest kingdom. And
I think it is no worser an house than mine own." Styrbiorn showed the King the great sword that hung at his
thigh, the same which the King had given him when he
went first abroad three years ago. The King asked if
that were a good sword. Styrbiorn said it was the best
of swords. He said he had had no other sword with
him in battle all these years, and it was better now than
at the first. He said it seemed to him that if he should
lose that sword he should lose all his good luck. "It
is like enough," said the King, "that there is somewhat
of me in that sword, who gave it thee. And like
enough my good will goeth with it, and maketh it do
good for thee."

The King sent Earl Wolf now in embassage to King Harald Gormson to bespeak his daughter in marriage for Styrbiorn. King Harald at first boggled at this, saying she was promised to the Wend-King. Yet in the end he was fain to own that this was yet but talked on and naught settled nor agreed yet; and when he saw how much King Eric was set upon the match, and bethought him too that the Swede-King's friendship should profit him well, and that Styrbiorn withal was an ill foe to quarrel with, and that Jomsburg lay at his own door too, in the end he gave Earl Wolf the answer he would have, and promised to send her to Upsala with as short delay as might be. And yet it was with little good will that he consented in this; for there weighed ever on his mind (like as weigheth a surfeit of tough meat on the belly that cannot deal with it) the memory of Styrbiorn's lording it over him last winter in Rois- keld, and of his saying (albeit in jest) that he would do of him and the Dane-realm as he should think fit.

It was not long before every man that was there in Upsala knew in his bones what manner of lord they had gotten now in Styrbiorn. And they saw very well that he had slipped his neck out of the collar, and was King already in deed, and bare him like a King and let all feel the weight of the might of him. And they marked too how those two, the King and Styrbiorn, were ever in company and were so glad of each other that it was a wonder to see; and most men praised these things and deemed well of their boding, but some wagged their heads in secret.

Only Thorgnyr came on an evening to the King, if he might sway him yet afore it should be too late. The King let him say his say. "You have heard, King," said that old man, "all that I have heard: you have seen what I see. He is altered not a whit. In Holmgarth and the east he hath overborne all. Jomsburg he holdeth in his hand. He hath brow-beat the Dane-King in his stead, and gone forth of the Dane-realm with threats and scornings. He is tied to no place, but all are tied to him. Save you only, there is none here in Sweden he entreateth in other wise than as his thrall or bondman. Give him all the world else, King, but give him not Sweden."

The King heard him out with so much good temper and patience it was a strange thing to see; then told him kindly 'twas but sawing in the air, since as touching his taking of Styrbiorn into kingdom his mind was set, and not Thorgnyr nor the Swede-folk nor all the North-lands might avail to shift it. Thorgnyr spake no more of that.

Well nigh every day Styrbiorn would still divert himself with wrestling and sporting with Moldi, that he had left with a thrall of his named Erland to tend for him whiles he fared abroad. Moldi was now come to his full growth: not big as other oxen, but exceeding sturdy and heavy. He was something cross-grained in his temper, and the thralls durst not touch him save

when he was in the mood for it. But he knew Styrbiorn when he first came home, and ran to him as soon
as he saw him, which was a wonder after these years.
And albeit there was no man else might handle him
except in his own time, with Styrbiorn he was as gentle
as a little calf might be.

On a day while Styrbiorn was a-wrastling with Moldi
on Upsala brink, Sigrid the Queen stood and looked
on their sport even as she had looked on it when he
wrastled with Moldi on Olaf's howe that morning after
Aki's slaying. When their bout was over and Styrbiorn stood up breathing hard, saw the Queen and gave
her greeting, she said, "Thy little ox is grown too big
for thee now, for all that men have given thee that
by-name of Styrbiorn the Strong. It is only to please
thee he letteth thee get the upper hand of him. If he
would, he could toss thee off like a ball."

"Why," said Styrbiorn, laughing, "I think thou'dst
not say so if thou couldst have felt the push of him as
I did now."

" 'Tis the same," said Sigrid, "with other folk, and
not thy little ox only. They must still be pleasing
thee, and serving thy turn. I think it is not good for
thee."

"I know not," said Styrbiorn, rubbing his face against
Moldi's soft grey hairy muzzle. "What think'st thou
on't, Moldi?"

"So thou weddest Thyri?" said the Queen after some
pause.

"So it is," said he.

"Thou hadst not the King thine uncle to do thy wooing for thee there," said she.

"He sent my foster-father," said Styrbiorn.

"The King thine uncle is a good wooer," said Queen Sigrid. "Yet ere this he hath gotten no for an answer."

Styrbiorn said, "Never that I heard tell of."

"There be things yet in the world that thou hast not heard tell of," said she, "for all thou knowest so much."

Styrbiorn said, "Little wit in a maid to say no to him."

"I will tell thee," said Sigrid. "It was I said no to him. But I will tell thee why I said no. It was because I thought he would woo me not for his own hand, but for another." So saying she looked swiftly at him; then, turning her eyes away, "I must learn thee somewhat in court terms," said she. "Thou shouldst now say: 'Tis a good wooer picketh wisely the best for himself."

Styrbiorn said, "Thou wouldst ever be mocking at me, Sigrid."

Sigrid reached out her hand to Moldi to lick. He licked hard and eagerly the hand and wrist and up the fair white arm of her, nuzzling back her sleeve with his sweet-breathing nose. She drew back her arm with a little shudder, then put her hand out again to fondle and play with his woolly jowl. "Thou and Thyri," she said, after a pause, "will be well matched. She hath ugly hair, I am told, but is very meek, and will do all thy bidding and say naught."

Styrbiorn was silent. But the Queen with her eyes bent still on Moldi, not on Styrbiorn, would still be talking. "I am in a manner thine aunt," said she. "I will give thee some wise counsel out of mine own wisdom. When thou art wed to Thyri, keep not wish-wives and bond-maids, o' thine uncle's fashion. And this I counsel thee for thine own comfort, kinsman Styrbiorn, not thy wife's. For doth it not seem to thee both just and fair: if one woman be not enough, why then must one man be?" With that she thrust Moldi from her, turned swiftly, and was suddenly gone.

Styrbiorn stood a minute looking after her as she went with swift and sure steps, daintily swaying from the hips, daintily gathering the skirt of her purple broidered gown to clear her ankles. As he so stood watching her, he was ware of Moldi that was nuzzling close to him now, busily licking his hand and arm. Suddenly he withdrew his arm, even as the Queen had hers, with a little shudder.

IX

A Banquet in Upsala

KING ERIC made ready now a great feast of many days, and summoned a Thing to be holden in the middle term thereof, at which Thing he was minded to make over and give unto Styrbiorn, his brother's son, with all lawful ceremonies and before the face of the Swedes in lawful Thing assembled, that half share of the kingly power in Sweden which King Olaf had held aforetime. And the feast was in honour as well of this greater matter as of Styrbiorn's betrothal unto Thyri the daughter of King Harald Gormson. Thyri was come now out of Denmark with a great and honourable company to bring her home to Upsala. The folk when they saw her deemed well of her and praised her beauty. That she loved Styrbiorn was clear as day, and men thought the two of them must have laid their plans for this in Denmark when Styrbiorn was with the King her father last winter.

The third night of their feasting was a banquet holden in the King's hall, and before that banquet was the troth-plighting of Styrbiorn and Thyri performed with due ceremony, and the banquet was the banquet of their betrothal, but the wedding should be after the Thing, when Styrbiorn should have taken kingdom.

Eric the King was set in his high seat on the upper bench, and the Queen at his right hand. Styrbiorn sat in the high seat on the lower bench over against the King, and Thyri his betrothed sat at his side. There was at that banquet every lord and man of mark that was of greatest account in all the land of the Swedes, both Earls and landed men and the King's counsellors and friends and the great men of his household, and the wives and kinswomen of these, and Styrbiorn's men that followed him out of Jomsburg: in all, so great a press of noble persons and those of their following who made shift to find place in every nook and corner of the hall, that never was so great a throng of folk gathered together in the King's house, and the thralls and serving men had much ado to serve meat and drink to all that company.

Helgi and Thorgisl and Thorir were sat cheek by jowl on the upper bench at the end nighest the door. They liked well of the good eats and drinks and made game together. They spoke softly so as they should not be overheard.

Thorgisl said, "Well fares he that sits quiet with his own. Sith Styrbiorn is come into kingdom now in our despite, let us drink and be glad and kick at the pricks no more."

"That is well said," said Helgi. "And yet, it dislikes me he should hold his chin so high, sitting there so glad, with his backside rooted in yonder high seat as though he were King already. If he be puffed up now so big, who shall abide to live under him when he shall be King indeed?"

"He thinketh," said Thorgisl, "on the Swede realm, which now lieth loose before him."

"Well," said Thorir, "so the ale runneth trill-lill down the throat, what need grieve us?"

Helgi drank and said, "None shall deny that Styrbiorn hath a pretty piece of flesh o' the right hand side of him. Would I were nearer, to mark if, spite o' that, his eye stray not toward the upper bench."

"A point eastward o' the King?" said Thorir: and they laughed. "'Tis not every man loveth the same meat, though, Helgi. I have marked the King look seldomer to-night of's own right hand than thereaway, to the crossbench."

"How? there?" said Helgi, craning forward over the board, and scanning the other women where they sat, seen dimly fair through the flicker and reek of fire and torchlight. "I see," he said, sitting back again and wiping the mead-froth from his moustachios with the back of his hand. His eyes wandered back toward the cross-bench: they glittered, and he ran his tongue over his lips.

"'Tis not every man hath his pick of such-like morsels," said Thorgisl. "He that had his pick, and picked not, should be a fool, to my thinking."

Thorir took him round the neck and said in his ear. "Helgi will not be slow to pick there, when his turn cometh: and little blame to him, think'st thou?"

"Is it any one?" said Thorgisl.

"Art thou blind?" said Thorir. "She, third from

the end: the King's latest bond-maid. O' the Erse King's blood, men say. If black women be ugly, there's argument for thee that foul is fair."

"Black women's the fashion to-night," said Thorgisl.

Helgi was yet licking his lips and shifting uneasily in his seat, his eyes yet on the black-haired damosel on the cross-bench. Looking round and seeing his comrades' laughing gaze upon him, he squared his shoulders, crammed his mouth with mutton, hailed the cupbearer for more drink, and said through his munchings, "Women's but cattle: one's like another, when all's said and done."

"So much the better for thee," said Thorir; "for I think thou'lt have to wait a weary while for this one."

Helgi drank and spat. "O, the trolls take thee and thy talk," he said.

"Thorgnyr receiveth all this wondrous calm," said Thorgisl after a time. "What if we have but mistook him all this while?"

"Never think it," said Helgi, looking up the table to where that old man sat, near the King. "Sometimes the sea will moan in a calm. I hear it now, methinks."

The hall was hung with outlandish hangings, curtains of rich crimson stuff and cloth of gold and broidered work brought out of Micklegarth or Garthrealm or the Western Isles, plunder of war or gifts of peace and tribute made to Styrbiorn by kings and lords that he had brought under him; and these treasures he had given now to the King his uncle, so many and rich and goodly as had not heretofore been seen, not one tenth the number nor goodliness, in the realm of Sweden. And there were plates of gold and great cups and breakers and goblets of gold and silver, rough with jewels and beautifully enchased, that made the rude, smoke-darkened and ponderous boards of the long tables blossom, like the brown earth in spring, with shining splendours. But the magnificence and glory of that banquet had root not in the fair setting only of gold and jewels and gorgeous tissues and weapons hung on the walls and armour glinting, but in the living presence and splendour of the men and women that feasted in that pomp: Eric the King, his youth come back upon him, eating and drinking and making merry, oftenest with his eye on Styrbiorn that sat there over against him in the beauty of his youth and strength; and that young affianced bride of Styrbiorn's, white-skinned and with night-dark hair, quiet, with eyes and ears only for him; and opposite, on the King's right hand, that fair young Queen of his. She too was quiet. The lids drooped over her dark eyes that looked out like some animal's eyes, profound and of doubtful import, under shadowing lashes, unsounded pools. Her face was flushed. Her red-gold hair, swept back in heavy shimmering and luxurious masses, shadowed her brow on either side, and was gathered and coiled again under strings of jewels darkly sparkling. Her gown was of silk, a treasure of untold price out of the land of the Greeks, deep purple and purfled with gold. There was a strange and disturbing grace in her quiet pose and carriage, as if the fair and lovely body of her with the burning fire of its beauty pierced the rich attire that hid it, giving to every silken fold and to every glittering gem a warm and breathing loveliness as of very flesh and blood. And yet her lord, sitting there at handreach, had eyes and mind, as it appeared, only for his nephew, if it were not for a side-long glance now and again at that newest damosel of his on the cross-bench. Styrbiorn for his part had eyes for all, merry of heart and at ease and at peace, as for that while, with all the world.

Now it began to be late, and men fell to telling of stories, and later on to man-matching. But the King made them give over this, deeming it likely to turn out too little peaceable a game in such a company as was there, being not of one land nor of one allegiance but of two or three. And he bade instead a skald of his sing them somewhat, whether some lay or drapa. "And best of all, some old love-song, sith this is a betrothal feast to-night." So the skald stood forth and in obedience to the King spake forth that song which men call the Hell-ride of Brynhild, in manner following—

The Ogress speaks

Hold! for thou gettest gangway never
Thorough this grit-built garth of mine.
Should better beseem thee to broider at home

Than to woo another's wedded lord.
What cam'st thou to woo from Valland hither
O fickle head, unto house of mine?
Gold lady, thou hast, (and thou list to know),
Those milk-white hands of man's blood washen.

Brynhild speaks

Braid not me therefor, O Bride of the Stone,
Though I of old did a-viking fare.
I shall be still the stronger called
Of us twain, whereso our tale men know.

The Ogress speaks

Thou, O Brynhild, Budli's daughter,
For an omen of ill on earth wast born:
The children of Giuki a-gley thou smotest,
And their good house didst hurl in wreck.

Brynhild speaks

I shall tell thee a true tale,
O nothing knowing (if know thou wilt):
What guerdon I had of Giuki's heirs—
To be reft of my true-love and troth-forlorn.
I was with Heimir in Hlymdale of old:
Seasons eight I sat there in joy.
Twelve winters had I (if wist thou wilt)
Ere oath I sware to any prince.
All they hight me in Hlymdale of old
Hild the Helm'd, whoso knew me.
Then let I, in the land of the Goths,

149

Helm-Gunnar the old to Hell go down:
To Aud's young brother I brought the glory:
Over wroth waxed Odin with me for that.
He lock'd me with shields in Skatalund,
Red shields and white; rim touch'd rim:
Bade he then that man break my slumber,
Who in the wide world wist not of fear.
About my stately southern hall
High he let blaze the bane of woods:
Bade he then only over it ride
Him who should get me that gold that 'neath **Fafnir** lay.
Riding on Grani, the good gold-scatterer
Came to my fosterer's famous steadings:
A viking better beyond all other
Deem'd they him in the host of the Danes.
Slept we and abode in one bed together,
As though he my brother born had been:
Not an hand of either drew nigh to other,
Eight nights long of our lying so.
Upbraided me Gudrun, Giuki's daughter,
That I had slept in Sigurd's arms;
Then wist I this clear which I would not wist:
That they had beguil'd me in bridegroom-getting.
World without end in woe and anguish
Must mankind and womankind quicken and live.
Now shall we twain never part,
Sigurd and I.—So sink thou: sink!

Now all were silent listening while the skald spake
that lay, for he spake it well and in a manner to touch
men's hearts. Styrbiorn sat still, harkening attentively;

and while he harkened his gaze was bent on Sigrid the Queen, where she sat over against him at the King's right hand. She sat there as heretofore looking down, so that her eyes were hid under their long lazy lashes. One arm of her rested on the table before her, toying with a fallen cup. Now Styrbiorn was held with the music of that song, and his thoughts within him were on the sadness of the song, so that, looking on the Queen, he saw not her, but in imagination that Queen of old time, Brynhild. So watching, he heard, as in a dream, the skald's sounding voice:

> Thou, O Brynhild, Budli's daughter,
> For an omen of ill on earth wast born:
> The children of Giuki a-gley thou smotest,
> And their good house didst hurl in wreck.

And as the song went on, Styrbiorn thought in himself: Brynhild? Why was she to blame for it? It was Odin set that fire about her, and that weird upon her. And that was Sigurd that rode through the fire. And yet, it was not to Sigurd that she was wed, but to Gunnar, son of King Giuki: and Sigurd wedded not her, that was his right love, but Gudrun instead, King Giuki's daughter. And then Brynhild slew herself on Sigurd's funeral pyre. It is a strange unlucky tale, and not easy for a man to tell the rights and wrongs of it. And now she is riding down the cold and stony way of Hell, and this Ogress would plague her now and hold her back from Sigurd.

In that study, and still looking with bodily eye on Queen Sigrid, he saw in her now in his mind's eye Brynhild in her free and glorious time, "Hild the Helm'd," the Valkyrie, Odin's shield-may. Like as in a trance he watched and marked, with wondrous clearness yet with a mind removed and dispassionate, the proud-curved luxurious lips half-open; the white throat of her, strong and delicate; the bosom of her, pressed a little, as it rose, against the edge of her gown, then as it fell leaving a hollow that opened on sweet unseen depths of softness and beauty. His inward gaze moved downward, unhindered by the table that stood in the way of his bodily sight; downward to the jewelled girdle, the byrny's skirt where it shaped its close-lying texture of shining interwoven rings of iron about the large rondure of her hips.

The skald spake the words:

> A viking better beyond all other
> Deem'd they him in the host of the Danes.

And Styrbiorn seemed in himself to be drowned yet deeper in the song, so that himself too was lost in it, and that which meant Sigurd meant him.

Then, at the words, "Upbraided me Gudrun, Giuki's daughter," he looked up: met, for the first time, Sigrid's glance, and became on the instant like a man drunk. He sat staring with eyes wide open into her eyes that, wide open too and unblinking, looked full in his. Then the Queen looked away. Styrbiorn heard, as if from afar off, Thyri whispering in his ear some trifle of lovers' talk. The gallop of his blood shook him so fiercely that he might not trust himself with speech. He reached out his hand to the mighty jewelled goblet before him, brimming with the froth of mead, and emptied it at a draught.

X

Broken Meats in Upsala

STYRBIORN slept the night after that banquet a sleep tumultuous with visions. In sleep, he rode a swift horse through lands silent and unpeopled, white with moonlight. He rode now through fires, as it were Brynhild's fiery girdle about Skatalund, and now down deep wooded valley-slopes of darkness, where the young leafage brushed his hair and lips and hands as he passed. Then, in the swirling about of the visions which belonged to that unquiet slumber, he seemed to behold suddenly Sigrid the Queen naked before him in a whiteness of blinding brilliance; with the glory of which sight, sleep broke, and he opened his dazzled eyes on lamp-light, and on Sigrid indeed in very presence standing beside his bed, but cloaked in her great scarlet cloak lined with swansdown.

She stood there by his feet, holding the lamp high. Her eyes were large and shining. Beholding him awake, she said, "I slept ill, and the whim took me to see if thou didst sleep to-night. I would not have waked thee." Her breath caught as she spoke.

Styrbiorn rose sharply on his two elbows. His eyes, broad awake now, were fixed on her. And there was in that look, and in the whole frame of him, a tenseness like as is in a bow-string stretched. His face, flushed with sleep, took while he looked a yet darker red.

"This would I know," he said, and his speech came hoarse and stumbling: "is it with the King's leave thou goest o' these night-walkings?"

Sigrid's mouth hardened. She gave him an odd look from half-closed eyelashes, then, daintily as a sea-gull settles on the sea, sat down at the far end of the bed. Styrbiorn's stillness was like the stillness of great clouds brooding before the lightning.

After a little he said, "Come nearer."

Sigrid marked his voice, and the look of him. These things gave her a delicate pleasure, as of dangerous steering round a rocky headland in a strong sailing breeze blowing on the land. "O no," said she. "I can hear thee very well so."

Styrbiorn moved a little. "Why needest thou have waked me out of my dream? Shall I not have atonement of thee for that, Sigrid? Shall I tell thee," he said, and his voice came like that light and sudden wind that sets a-quiver the leaves before a storm, "what I was a-dreaming on?" With that, he would have caught her into his arms; but she was a wary steersman, too swift for this gust of his, sudden though it was, and was leapt up and out of the door ere he could reach her. Styrbiorn, barefoot, guided by the leaping flicker of the wind-blown lamp, overtook her at her own door, flung himself in betwixt door and doorpost before she might shut him out, and had her in a moment alone with him in her own chamber, trapped.

The Queen stood facing him between the bed-head

and the wall.   She had set the lamp on a shelf, shoulder-
high on her left, and stood there rigid, cloaked to the
eyes in her great scarlet mantle, her eyes fierce and
bright, like some beautiful beast brought to bay, her
breath coming and going in pants.   She did not speak.
Styrbiorn abode some paces off, by the closed door.   He
reached a hand behind him, fumbling for the bolt,
found it, and shot it softly home.   He abode there
silent, his hand still on the bolt, leaning towards her as
the setting moon leans towards the sea.   So for a minute's space they face one another, Styrbiorn and the
Queen, alone with the lamp-light and its shifting shadows: with the velvet dark (with here and there a faint
star shimmering) that filled the window above the
Queen's bed with the silence of night, so deep that each
seemed to hear the other's heart-beats: night, that is of
kin with those shadowy-visaged and iron-handed Fates
that lay men at their length: summer night, and the
glittering of her eyes and his in the beams of the watch-
ful lamp.

Styrbiorn came a step nearer to her, his gaze fixed,
like a sleep-walker, saying, hardly above his breath,
"Sigrid."   She neither spoke nor moved, but abode as
if fascinated.   Like the passing shadows of the moon,
so silently he drew towards her, or like some motion
of those grey Fates, or of things drawn by them blindly.
He was kneeled now at her feet, his arms locked about
her above her knees.   The Queen rested motionless,
only he felt the quivering of her flank under the rich

mantle where his cheek was pressed. Styrbiorn lifted
his eyes to her face; and now time past and time to
come went for him clean away out of mind and car-
ing, so that he was ware now no longer of any other
thing save only of her: the perfume of her presence,
her lips that parted a little, her eyes that looked down
on him dark and wide. His hands reached upward
and, as if afraid all should on the motion vanish in air,
paused, scarcely touching her either shoulder. She, still
gazing on Styrbiorn out of her eyes' unsounded darks,
suddenly let slip with a noble and divine grace her
great red mantle, and stood there in her white loveliness before him.

The night wore now, and the stars moved on, and
those unseen powers which weave the web of destiny
threw the shuttle yet again, and Styrbiorn, with his wits
now awake again, looked and beheld in the lamp-light
stretched at his side there Sigrid the Queen, and, in his
mind's eye, that which he had this night accomplished.
He leaped from the bed.

The Queen, startled so out of her sweet and pleasant
dreams, sat up, first in amaze: then, meeting her lover's
wild and unfriendly regard, her proud face darkened
and she rendered him back look for look in that kind.
He turned with a sudden blundering twist of the body;
but she was, as for this time, the swifter, and, leaping
up and catching her cloak about her, stood betwixt him

and the door. He swerved side-long from her and came heavily against the wall, face to the wall, his eyes buried in his great hands.

The Queen beheld him awhile in silence. "It is likely thou art some churl's son," said she at length; "or some changeling. No man of kingly blood would carry it thus, after honours the like of which I've done thee: more's the pity."

Styrbiorn moved like a blinded man towards the door; then, finding her in the way, gave back a pace. Then he said, yet with eyes averted and in alien and hard tones half-choked, "Let me go, Sigrid."

"I'll let thee go," said she, "when thou speakest to me like my noble kinsman, not like a base-born thrall."

For a moment he paused as if doubting what were best to do, then lifted up his head and strode forward as if he were minded to thrust her aside by force. At hands'-reach he halted. The ghastliness of his look as he stood and looked upon her took from her for a minute all power of thought or motion. Then he opened his mouth and said, "What have I to do with thee, a faithless bitch?"

With that, he turned from her, catching in his two hands the pillars of the bed. Under the grip of his hands and the weight of him flung between them the great oak pillars shook and creaked. He turned again, dazed yet with this nightmare, steadying himself yet

161

with one hand by the pillar of the bed. He looked at her now with eyes like some dog's eyes asking to be let out: naught else matters.

But the Queen faced him, back to the door, staring. Under the injury of those words she had moved not an eyelid. But instant by instant she seemed stonier grown; her face whitened, even to the lips; and then the blood flooded back terribly. She said in a low tone, the words even and steady like water dropping and clear as the clicking of blades, "But this shall be thy death, then." Therewith so loud shrieked Sigrid the Queen that the cups rang on the wall and the geese screamed in the King's garth.

She gave him way now: but he was not quicker in the doorway than those women of hers, hearing this larum, and others running. Styrbiorn, thrusting past them like one straught of his right wits, butted into old Thorgnyr three paces without the Queen's chamber-door. He swerved past the old man, and Helgi caught at him. He smote Helgi so good a whirt on the ear as laid him out senseless. Styrbiorn came so to his own chamber, yet not so well but that Thorgnyr and Helgi and some four or five women of the Queen's had seen him in such sort rush out from the Queen's bed-chamber.

Eric the King came now, roused by that great cry, cloaked and with bare sword in one hand and a lamp in the other, along the passage to the Queen's chamber. They gave back all before him to right and left: not one, neither Thorgnyr nor any other, took heart to speak word to him, but gave back and let him by. He came in, looked on her an instant, then shut to the door behind him. Sigrid fell down at his feet and clasped him about the knees in a great passion of tears. The King suffered that to have its course. Choking and sobbing she let him understand little by little to what vile use his darling nephew, lust-burned and ale-heated, had by violence turned her. The King heard all out, silent and without sign or stir, looking down the while on her head bowed and shaken with her sobbing and crying, on the nape of her neck where the first little hairs shadowed the white skin with their prettily curled growth, and, where her cloak opened at the throat, on that sweet and shadowy place where her breasts pressed one against the other like two doves perched together on the edge of a roof. When she had told her tale, she looked up in his face and cried and said, "Lord, why didst thou leave me?"

Like a great tower and big the King stood over her. He said nothing: only lifted up his jaw a little and so stood looking steadily before him over her head, with set face. Sigrid, frighted with his coldness, rose up, clinging her arms now about his neck, shivering and weeping with her face hidden on the King's breast. Stone still he stood. His face looked drawn and hard, awful to look on, unsearchable as the brow of night, and sad like the sea under a winter dawn. At length, coming out of that study, he looked down at her again, gently loosed her hands from about his neck and without word said went from the chamber. Sigrid, looking at his face, deemed it wholesomer to speak no word but let him go.

A bleak greyness of morning began now to pale their lamps and the last embers of the long fires in the King's hall. In a little while there came a man to Thorgnyr from the King bidding him come and see the King straightway. Thorgnyr went, and found the King sitting armed in his chair with a drawn sword laid across his knees. The King looked at him a long time in silence. Thorgnyr stood with head bowed. At length the King said, "Let me see thy face, Thorgnyr." That old man raised his eyes and looked the King in the face. After a minute the King spake again and said, "Forty years hast thou been my man. It is well that thou shouldst know my mind." And he said, "Of these things that have this night befallen I will have no man speak to me, neither thou nor another, on pain of death. For the Queen, every woman should be forgiven once. For Styrbiorn, thou shalt go thyself and find him and say unto him that he shall have free way out of the Swede-realm so he be gone this very day. But if ever he shall come into the land again so long as I be alive, or shall come anigh me, that shall be his death."

Thorgnyr said naught, looking on the King from under the dark eaves of his brows. His lean hands twitched a little. Then he spoke, "You have some-

164

times thought I played for mine own hand, Lord, and not for yours. Will you not see him?"

"If I should see him," answered the King, "that should be his death. Go thou, and do my bidding."

Thorgnyr went out from before the King. There was great stir throughout the house, and a noise of horses in the King's garth. Thorgnyr went out into the garth and came upon Styrbiorn as he went a-horseback, and his Jomsburgers were mounting round about him on every side. Thorgnyr came close to Styrbiorn, so that none might hear save the twain of them, and gave him the King's message neither adding aught to it nor taking aught away. Styrbiorn had the look of a man stupid for sleeplessness during many nights. Thorgnyr, knowing not for sure if he had heard the message aright, spake it over again word by word. But Styrbiorn answered and said, "I heard thee very well. Thou hast gotten the goal, then. What need to trattle more on't?" Therewith he swung his leg into the saddle and, without looking back or giving further heed to Thorgnyr, rode with his men out of the King's garth and out of Upsala southward to the sea.

XI

Jomsburg Sea-Walls

STYRBIORN stood on the outer sea-wall at Jomsburg while they brought his fleet in through the seagates: a tricky work, seeing there was a heavy sea running, and the last part worst of all, for it was now long past sunset, and their only light torch-light and the moon shining fitfully through flying racks of vapour. But it was by his command; and there was that in his eye since they sailed out of the Low three days gone that made his folk count it safer to risk the smashing may be of one ship or two sooner than meddle with him. Styrbiorn stood there in his war-gear, wearing under his gold-edged byrny that Greek kirtle of cramoisy silk and gold which the princess of Holmgarth had given him in days gone by, and about his middle that mighty silver girdle with horse-headed serpents intertwined at every link, the same which he had taken from about Jomala's middle in the temple amid the wolds of Kirialaland, and the barbarous people had watched in vain to see earth gape for him that wrought so impiously; and from that girdle hung the heavy two-edged sword, Eric's gift, wherewith he had made so many famous conquests: the same wherewith he had fought and prevailed against Palnatoki's self when first he came to Jomsburg. He was bareheaded and, according to his common wont in these days, without cloak or mantle, so that the glory of his arms was naked to the eye, and the breadth of his shoulders, that cast about him, in their proud shapely poise, a mantle of more kingliness than royal and costly stuffs might ever shed about a king.

Fierce and sullen was the countenance of Styrbiorn, yet quiet, as of a fierce beast charmed with music, as he watched that dance of the rolling surges sweeping and pausing and falling and rising again: Ran's eternal children leading their round as if in sad ceremonial observance of some divinity hidden apart, removed from all knowledge or communion of human kind; and listened to the swelling roar of the breaker as it rode on, the thud and thunder of its fall, and the grinding hiss of the shingle in the back-wash, as if wrath, which is older than the world and older than the Gods, drew in its breath once again, pondering some greater mischief.

Stepping back to avoid a wave that flung itself with more than ordinary violence against the sea-wall and tossed high above it a wild white man of spray, Styrbiorn found himself in the arms of Biorn Asbrandson that was come up behind him unheard.

"What fiend bewitched thee?" said Biorn. "Could'st thou not have beached 'em in the firth where calm water is and a sheltered shore? There's one stove in but now by the gate, and men drowned, like enough: we cannot tell i' this windy dark."

"Let them drown, then," said Styrbiorn; "and thou too, unless thou mend thy talk." He swung round away from Biorn, and the great sword at his side, Eric's gift, clanked against his thigh. He took it in his two hands, peered at it for a moment in the glimpsing moonbeams as if at some strange thing, then unfastened it sheath and all from his girdle and sent it hurtling into the sea. "And that, afore all," he said.

Biorn, being a man of sense, held his peace.

The last ship was in. After a while Styrbiorn, still in his former posture watching the endless procession of surges, said in hard toneless accents, "Shall I tell thee what I did in Sweden?"

"Am not I thy brother?" said Biorn.

Styrbiorn said, "I dallied with a whore, and I lost a kingdom."

Biorn, who knew when silence is best, said nothing.

Styrbiorn lifted his eyes to the moon, high over Wendland to the east, that showed like a dead queen's face, white and forlorn, behind a drifting waterish veil of broken cloud that turned all the sky to tarnished silver. Nearer at hand, through a lower level of air, woolly clouds black as coal were charioted by the tearing wind one by one across the face of the moon. Each as it passed seemed to catch and retain some tincture of her brightness, and fled down the wind eastward mantled with a darkness less pitchy than before. Here and there for an instant a star beamed down.

Styrbiorn said, "I lied to thee. Thus it was: I have foully belied a Queen, and lost that which all the world and the kingdoms of the world might not avail to purchase again for me."

Biorn, thinking in himself that such speeches are but as so many catches and scrabblings of a man over head and ears in water, said nothing, but gripped him by the hand. Styrbiorn kept the hand in his, tightening his iron grasp upon it whenever it offered to move away, and standing in all other respects motionless for a long time with feet firm planted wide apart, like some colossus brooding above the flood. Biorn, his hand in his, felt the throb of his veins, not less thunderous nor less deep-drawn from the ultimate springs of life and fate than that thunder of waters about Jomsburg sea-wall, the pulse of the elemental sea.

Stybiorn said at last, "Men of lore will tell thee that adulterers when they come to die must wander in streams of venom, at the strand of corpses remote from the sun, in that castle which is woven of the spines of snakes. Is that true, foster-brother, thinkest thou?"

Biorn answered, "I do not know."

"Thou art mine elder by ten year, and shouldst know more than I," said Styrbiorn.

For a great while Styrbiorn was silent, following with his eye the mighty rhythm of the waves, where one after another stormed up the wall, clutched, and fell, and swept back to sea; and every wave as it plunged back seaward from the wall met another wave coming on, and like young living things in their boisterous sport the two waves meeting clasped and tumbled one another, clashed together with a shout and reared high in the air, a single sudden pillar of flashing foam. Then he said, "Snorri the Priest drove thee out of Iceland because of a woman."

"Not drove me," said Biorn. "I went, though."

Styrbiorn turned sharp upon him, set a hand on either shoulder of him, drew him close, and looked him close in the eye. He said, "Follow me, and I shall show thee wonders. There is no good thing under sun or moon, Biorn. He that will follow me shall get no good by it. There is no good for me to give him, in all the world. But dominion he shall get, and power, and this withal: that when my foot is on the neck of the King of Danes, and of King Burisleif, and the great King in Micklegarth, and— No more; but his foot that will follow me shall be there beside my foot, 'stead of his neck beside theirs."

"Thou art a blasphemer," said Biorn. "And I think thou art fey."

"Is that all thou hast to tell me?" said Styrbiorn.

Biorn answered and said, "There is this, too: that I will not leave thee nor forsake thee so long as both thou and I be alive."

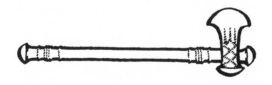

XII

The Cowing of the Dane-King

THE lords of Jomsburg came in now from their summer viking. Styrbiorn would speak to no man of those things which had come about in Upsala at summer's end; but they remained not hidden, for they that had fared with him into Sweden told it to their messmates, and it was in most men's minds that he was not likely to sit quiet under that shaming.

All that winter Styrbiorn abode in Jomsburg. He was moody and ill to do with. Biorn was with him winter-long, but the rest of them went every one to his own place: Sigvaldi and his brethren to Skaney, Bui and Sigurd to the old man Veseti their father in Borgundholm, and the rest accordingly. Palnatoki, ere that he went home into Fion, took Styrbiorn apart and said, "Few be they that can stand alone. I would have thee remember this: whatsoever thou art minded to do or whithersoever to fare next summer, we will lend thee aid as thumb serves finger." Styrbiorn gripped him by the hand.

Styrbiorn grew blacker of mood as winter deepened. He would be oftenest alone; out of doors all day long in the wildest weather, walking hours together on the sea-walls; rowing out to sea sometimes in a boat alone; once or twice, in weather when no boat could live long, swamped and swimming ashore out of seas which no man, save by luck, could look to win out of alive. Other whiles he would go alone upon the mainland, ranging among the hills and sea-cliffs. Now the thrall Erland, at Styrbiorn's riding from Upsala, had bethought him to bring Moldi and ship him aboard and carry him south to Jomsburg. For it seemed to him that his lord was now leaving behind him in the Swede-realm many a thing should grieve his heart to lose it, and that here was one thing might be saved for him and that he should be glad of, albeit he had no mind as for that while neither for that nor for naught else beside. And so it was that when Styrbiorn fared alone upon the mainland, Moldi would ever follow some way behind him. But Styrbiorn seemed neither to see him nor to know he was there, taking, if he saw him indeed, no more note of him than he might take of his own shadow. In such times, not Moldi only shadowed him unnoticed, but Biorn also was wont to follow him all day afar off with a band of men, lest he should be set upon by the Wends. But, whether because they were ware of Biorn and his company at hand, or for their old fear of Jomsburg and of Styrbiorn, or (which was scarce reason enough) because peace was between King Burisleif and the Jomsburgers, the Wends held off from them.

When Yule-month was well past and the days began to lengthen, Styrbiorn began to come out some little from his black and sullen frame of mind. On an evening as they walked on the wall in the bright beams

178

of the westering sun, he spake and said to Biorn his foster-brother, "There was one thing I was wrong to leave behind me. And I have not missed him until now."

"What was that?" said Biorn.

"That was Moldi."

"Moldi," said Biorn, "hath followed thee all winter long. Thou hast never all winter walked abroad but he was behind thee."

"Thou mockest me," said Styrbiorn, staring at him.

"It is very truth I tell thee," said Biorn. " 'Twas thy man Erland brought him for thee out of Sweden."

"Erland!" said Styrbiorn. "And thou!" And he turned away his face.

Now was winter over, and Jomsburg filled again, and Palnatoki according to his wont held council with the lords of the Jomsburgers to determine of their summer's work. So they were met together on the sea-wall overlooking the open sea and the sea-gates and the harbour and the ships. Palnatoki took his seat on a high buttress top that jutted a little above the wall: Styrbiorn sat at the right hand of Palnatoki and Sigvaldi at the left, and the rest sat or stood round about on either side. Every man of them was helmed and byrnied and armed as if for battle, for in such array held they ever their councils of war.

When they were set, Palnatoki spake among them: "That hath been our custom until now, that I should ask each man in turn what seemeth likeliest and best to him, and what rede he hath to lay before us. But this summer I think we shall choose the rather to hear what Styrbiorn will do. For I think there is no man here in Jomsburg who will not wish to put aside his own enterprise, how needful soever it be, and give aid to Styrbiorn."

So said Palnatoki, and they took his saying well. Only Sigvaldi leaned closer to Palnatoki and spake somewhat in his ear. "I care not for that," said Palnatoki: "I will have no conditions." And he said aloud, "And this is our mind, as it seemeth to me, that we shall give Styrbiorn aid not here nor there, nor for this or that, but freely and for what thing soever he will take in hand."

Sigvaldi bit his lip but kept silence. And now he with the rest rose up, and every man that was at that council bared sword now and clashed iron on iron, sword on shield, crying aloud that he would aid Styrbiorn.

Styrbiorn swept his eye round from man to man. For a moment he scarce seemed able to speak word. Then in his eager and halting utterance he said, " 'Bare is back without brother behind it.' And I see that shall not be said of me. And now there is but one man and one country I will not bear war against: every land else, but not against the Swede-King. Many will think wonders at this, but I will for no sake bear war against King Eric. This I say, that you may know. But if

180

I fight not against him, fight I must with someone, or
I shall burst."

"What's this?" said Bui then. "Must thou be cast
out o' the Swede-realm and thine own lawful right for
a wench sake? And were it possible for any shame-
swollen toad to have the spit-proof face to outlive this
disgrace, and not make garters of the guts of him that
put it on us?"

Styrbiorn met his scowling and staring look with that
smile with which, once his mind was set on anything,
he was wont to receive advice or protest or upbraiding.
"I will not fight with the Swede-King," said he.

Bui said, "Thou dost jest with us. This is but to
try us. Come, I'll go with thee. He shall find a hath
laid for a pickrell and caught a fire-drake. And I'll
ask no guerdon but this, that I may lay in the first
brand at the burning of Upsala."

"I'll give thee quarry enough, Bui," said Styrbiorn,
"but never that." Men might see, for all his holding
of himself in hand, that this talk tried his temper over
much.

Sigvaldi spake: "We have promised Styrbiorn this,
to follow and uphold him this summer. And methinks
there is little wisdom in this, to egg him on to so un-
hopeful and bad an enterprise as that should be, to go
up against the King o' the Swedes in Upsala. For
many a man would find it a hard thing and an ill to
keep to his oath, were it to draw us into such-like folly."

But the more part of them were of Bui's mind, that

they would back Styrbiorn, were it in this or in aught else beside.

After this Palnatoki spake to each apart, and said it would be best for men to speak no more to Styrbiorn of the ill turn things had taken betwixt him and the Swede-king, and most of all say naught, as Bui had said, of bearing war against the King; "For that is furthest from his mind, and the mere thought thereof is like a spark to a vetch-stack, to light up his grief and ruth anew."

Styrbiorn sailed east now with the whole power of the Jomsburgers, and made war far and wide in the east countries and laid under him there many kings and folk both of the main-land and of the isles, in such sort that the terror of the name of Jomsburg was upon all the dwellers in those lands beyond aught that had been heard of aforetime. For Styrbiorn, sailing oft in raids and onslaughts with but a few ships, seemed to run all danger out of breath, nor might any host hold ground against him nor escape his onset. And the report did fly of him throughout Wendland and Garthrealm and Estland and all those lands of the eastern seas, that he was no man, but a troll which irons bite not; and under that fear went his enemies against him into battle. But as many as he overcame and conquered he bound to him with oaths and treaties and obliged men far and wide to host-faring with him. And men marked, too, this strange thing of him, that, for all the awe and fear folk had of him, yet there was a scarce a man that once spake with him and knew him face to face but was glad ever after to do his will and be his man. For he drew men to him as the lodestone draws iron.

After that, he bare war into Wendland, holding it time that the Wends should stand no longer in doubt whether Jomsburg, that was planted on their land's edge, were theirs or its own. But here gathered against him the war-rush of the Wends, and therewithal King Burisleif, having with him so huge a throng of fighting men as outmanned the Jomsburgers by five or six to one, seized the river banks of both sides below the fleet that had rowed far upstream into the inland parts. And the Wends cast booms athwart the river, cutting off for the men of Jomsburg their way of flight, had that seemed best to them. Their battle there was of the hardest, and there fell many a man of either side, for the Wends were good fighters and the odds by common reckoning hopeless against the men of Jomsburg. Yet in the end, after a long day's battle, Styrbiorn won the day. These were his peace terms with King Burisleif, that Palna-toki should henceforth hold an Earl's name and dignity, and the Wends should be at peace henceforth with them of Jomsburg and acknowledge them for their friends and allies, and should aid and comfort them every way they might from that day forth. King Burisleif gave Styrbiorn great store of gifts and trea-

sures, and bound himself to fetch Styrbiorn ships and
men to go a-warring with him whensoever he should
call for them.

It now drew toward midsummer. They brought
home their spoil to Jomsburg and bestowed it there and
set their gear in order. Then Styrbiorn said, "That
will I now, that we sail in west-viking. And first, into
Denmark."

It was easy to see that Palnatoki liked not well of this
rede. "A Dane am I by kin," said he, "and my home
is in Fion. And plainly I hold not myself for a bigger
man than King Harald Gormson, seeing I was content
to be fosterer of his son. Give us not too hard a choice."

At that, Styrbiorn looked black on him for an instant.
Then his brow cleared. "I ought not to have asked
thee for this, Palnatoki," he said, and took him by the
hand. "Let be, then. We will think on some other
way."

"That is generous in thee," said Palnatoki. "And
that is but what we have learnt to look for in thee,
we that be thy friends. But now I will not be be-
hindhand with thee in friendship, nor use thee so un-
handsomely, seeing I swear oath to aid thee. And thou
shalt have thy way, be it even into Denmark."

So this was now determined on. Only it seemed
good to Palnatoki that he should not himself be with
them on this sailing, thinking that, when the time
should come, the King should then the easier be brought
to eat out of his hand if he should have had no share

in the putting of force upon him. So this was their rede, that Palnatoki with those sons of Strut-Harald and one half of the whole fleet that was now in Jomsburg should sail again eastaway and withal raise more power in the east there, and be at tryst with Styrbiorn in Jomsburg the first full moon after midsummer. So might they thereafter all fare together a-warring until summer's end.

Styrbiorn, having with him Biorn and the sons of Veseti and the rest of the host, sailed now in westviking into Denmark and there made great unpeace. When he had gotten three victories in sea-fights there, he sailed through the Jutland sea into the Limfirth and found there the Dane-King and his host. The King deemed it not hopeful to fight with Styrbiorn, and they made peace there. King Harald had in those days a fair great house of his at Alaburg, and he bade Styrbiorn come ashore there and take guesting. Styrbiorn said yea to that, and now were the ships of King Harald and the ships of Styrbiorn some of them drawn up on the strand of the sea below Alaburg, while other some rode at anchor, for that was a windless haven and a wondrous good riding-place for ships. The King handselled peace to Styrbiorn before all the folk there, but they put off till the morrow all talk of terms and bargains.

That afternoon it so fell out that Styrbiorn, walking in the sun about the home-mead and whiling away the time with looking on the good byres and sheep-pens and on the fire-halls and bowers and other fair buildings that the King had in Alaburg, came on a sudden round a corner of the great hall face to face with Thyri, Harald's daughter. She was bare-headed and the sun shone in blue gleams amid the jet-black curls and folds of her hair. She wore a gown of dark-blue woollen stuff and a silken cloak, rich and costly, of like colour. She had in her arms a little furry rabbit that nestled against her bosom and, with long ears laid back, thrust its nose under her arm. It so befell that Styrbiorn was humming a tune and Thyri too was singing softly to her rabbit, rocking it and smiling to see it nestle so and to feel its soft nose nuzzling. So meeting, they stopped suddenly from their singing and halted as if each would have turned back to avoid the other, and their faces flushed red. Styrbiorn stepped aside now to let her pass. But Thyri stood still as if waiting for him to say somewhat. She stood looking down at the little rabbit in her arms, stroking its ears and head. After a little she looked up at him and said, "There was a foumart caught it, but I saved it."

Styrbiorn said nothing, meeting her gaze in an uneasy silence. Then on the sudden they both smiled.

That night the King made Styrbiorn and his folk good entertainment. Styrbiorn spake most to Thyri, and she was easy and open in her talk with him. There was no word nor look of hers that pointed to that bad night that had parted them in Upsala, but it was as if her mind had been wiped clean now of all knowledge and remembrance of it. And wondrous it seemed with what friendship she took up the threads of their days that had gone before, so that no dear brother and sister, meeting again after many years, might have known more familiarly the jests and likings each of other.

Suddenly he said to her, "Men have told me thou art to wed King Burisleif."

"So it is," said she, as if roused suddenly from some dream.

"Is that with thy good will?" asked Styrbiorn.

All her easy way with him was gone. She lifted her head proudly as if to say, what had he to do with these things? Then her eyes met his. She lowered her gaze and said, scarce to be heard, "No."

"It is an old man?" said Styrbiorn.

"So I am told," she said, soft as a breath.

They kept silence for a while. Then Styrbiorn said, "I did wrong. Is it too late?"

Thyri lifted her eyes full on his. "No," she said.

Next morning Styrbiorn and Harald the King went forth to speak together apart upon a bluff of rock that overlooks the strand of the sea below Alaburg. These were Styrbiorn's peace-terms that he laid before the King: that the Danes should fetch Styrbiorn an hundred ships full-manned to follow and fight for him in three great battles, and that he besides should have to wife Thyri, Harald's daughter.

It was easily seen that the King was not minded to have aught to do with such terms.

187

So now they talked on this for a long while, turning it over this way and that, but no whit the nearer were they agreed together. "That have I heard," said the King at length, "that thou hast been little of a tame horse to lead for thine unfriends. But this thou asketh passeth all reason, and I will not do it."

"That is ill, then," said Styrbiorn. "For so it is, King, that hereon hangeth all our friendship betwixt you and us Jomsburgers."

The King looked him in the eye. "I would have thee answer me this," he said: "Who art thou, that Jomsburg lieth in thy mouth? Let Palnatoki speak for Jomsburg, and thou for thyself."

Styrbiorn laughed. "Well," he said, "I will speak for myself."

"And I," said the King, "have given thee thine answer."

"But it is an answer I will not take," said Styrbiorn.

The King looked angry as a man might be. For a time he held his peace, then, suddenly looking up at Styrbiorn, "Would thou mightest go from hence," he said fiercely, "and all the fiends of hell go with thee. There was never ill words, let alone ill deeds, 'twixt me and Jomsburg, till that thou camest hither. With Palnatoki and every man else of Jomsburg I should lightly be set at one. Would I might never look upon thy face again."

Styrbiorn smiled. "I have tried your temper over much, King. And now I'm sorry for it. The ships

188

I will forgo. But to knit our friendship the closer you shall give me your daughter."

"That is not to be thought of," said King Harald. "Thou hast had thy chance of that, and little with my good will, when thine uncle backed thee. I scarce think he'll back thee again, though." With that, he gave Styrbiorn a lowering look. "Truly thou hast the front of a dog," said he: "'Be wary with ale and with another's wife.' When thou'st learnt that, come and ask me again for my daughter."

The hair of Styrbiorn's head rose up a little, and his face became dark as blood. "I' the mean time," said the King, "she is promised to King Burisleif. And the wedding is to be this summer."

"Is that with her good will?" said Styrbiorn.

"It is my will," said the King.

"Wilt thou leave it in her free choice?"

"I will not," said the King.

Styrbiorn came a pace nearer to Harald the King and stood over him like as one fighting dog stands a-bristling over another. "I love not talk and chat," said he; "yet, to please your whim, King, I have spent two hours a-talking. Here be no eavesdroppers. Thou seest under thy feet there my ships and thine. Think well: for this choice I give thee, either to stretch out thine hand and betrothe to me thy daughter, and swear friendship to me, and these hundred ships too; or if not, I will flit thee ashipboard this very night, over seas to Kirialaland or the Finn-heaths of Smaland or otherwhere, and de-

liver thee up to savage men shall shear off thy nose
and thine ears and draw out thy tripes for their dogs
to eat. Choose, then."

His words, tripping and stumbling, came like a clatter of weapons about the King's ears. The King looked
up in his eyes without blenching, a deadly look. A
dirty greyish pallor was on the King's cheek and brow:
his lips were drawn back, showing in a set grin his teeth
and gums and that ugly great tooth of his that jutted
forth like a wild swine's tusk blue and monstrous in the
left-hand corner of his mouth. His right hand was
clenched like iron on his sword-hilt, but his sword
abode safe home in the scabbard. When Styrbiorn had
ended there was deep silence, save for the faint sound of
the wash of the waves on the sea-shore below them.

"So it is, Styrbiorn," said King Harald at length,
"that thou art a strong man. But I think thy strength
shall one day over-reach itself. I' the mean season,
thou must have thy way, here as in what else besides.
But if thou wilt humour me so far, to forbear from
shaming me before mine own folk, that will seem somewhat."

"Then is the bargain made," said Styrbiorn. His
wrath was gone by like a squall in March, and that
good and merry look that his friends knew in him crept
like spring sunlight from his eyes and brow down to his
mouth. He reached out his hand. The King's hand
in Styrbiorn's grip was like a dead fish. Styrbiorn said,
"True it is, there is no witness of our bargain. Yet I

think thou'lt keep troth with me.   But I will have thine oath too, King."

The King sware by Christ and Mary.

"I'll have thee tied all ways," said Styrbiorn.   "Thou must now swear by Thor."

The King sware by Thor.

Styrbiorn said, "Now we understand one another, thou and I.   And now I shall think well of our friendship."

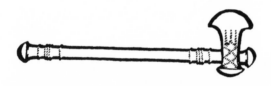

XIII

The Sailing of the Fleet

WHEN it was given out by what agreement King Harald and Styrbiorn were made friends men wondered much, thinking that here was a new strong wind set in, to blow so suddenly away that old standing bridal pact made with King Burisleif. The King's men for the most part thought that he had shown wisdom in these dealings, and in a day or two were all quarrels forgot that had arisen betwixt the Dane-folk and them of Jom; and most men accounted this to Styrbiorn. And they marked how even the King himself seemed, in outward show at least, of one mind with Styrbiorn and entreated him as he had been his very son. Styrbiorn and Thyri were wed now without more ado.

Now was the time come near for their keeping tryst with Palnatoki, and Styrbiorn sent Biorn Asbrandson his foster-brother to Jomsburg to let Palnatoki know they were with King Harald and how that affair had sped, so that Palnatoki might come now with all his power of fighting ships to Styrbiorn in Alaburg, instead of waiting for him in Jomsburg as they before determined. For this was in Styrbiorn's mind now, that they should sail that summer west over England's-main and lay under them those western lands. Men spoke well of the choice of land there, and the land was called a good land and worth the harrying.

In due time came Biorn back alone. He had this to say: that Palnatoki was there indeed in Jomsburg with his host, and had besides a great multitude of men and ships gathered from the east; but when he would have had these follow him to Alaburg, then said they all that they were come thither to Jomsburg to meet with Styrbiorn, and that they were not minded to go thence at any man's bidding until Styrbiorn should come to fetch them; but that when he should come, then they would go with him whithersoever he would, and do his commands. Styrbiorn saw there was naught for it but he must fare to Jomsburg. That was the tenth night now of their guesting with King Harald in Alaburg. They sat at supper, and Styrbiorn was glad and merry as he had not been these many months.

It was wonderful stormy weather that night, and it so befell that there was sailing by the Jutland coast a little north of the east mouth of the Limfirth a man of Iceland bound south out of the Swede-realm on a cheaping voyage. The wind and the sea drave his ship aland and she was broken in pieces in the shallows, but the skipper and his ship's company saved themselves and came ashore. That was about sunset. This chapman was named Worm Grimkelson. Oft had he sailed a-cheaping into the land of the Danes aforetime, and it was ever King Harald's wont to make him welcome. There was no dwellings of men thereabouts whereas Worm and his shipmates were come ashore, so they took this rede, to make haste to Alaburg and crave shelter of

Harald the King. They fell in with no man on their way thither through the wind and rain, and so it was that when Worm came into the hall and stood before the King and gave him greeting he knew not at all that these were Jomsburgers a-guesting there with King Harald, nor that Styrbiorn was there; nor was Styrbiorn known to him by sight nor any of those that were with him.

The King bade thralls look to Worm's men and give them to eat and drink, but for Worm himself the King let make room at the board. The King asked him was there good cheaping this year, and Worm answered it was better than some years and worse than others. The King asked whence they were come, and Worm answered they were come from Sigtun.

"Thou art the first man this year, Worm," said King Harald, "to come south hither out of the Swede-realm. What tidings hast thou to tell us thence? For I think it good sport to hear tales and tidings a-nights when men have eaten and supped."

The chapman answered and said, "There is naught newer, Lord, than that which befell last summer's end, when Styrbiorn the Strong was fled away out of Sweden because of King Eric, and the King let crown his young son Olaf joint King with him in Styrbiorn's stead. And he is called Olaf the Lap-King, because he was crowned a-sitting in his mother's lap, being but two winters old as is said. And this is in every man's mouth there, and is thought great tidings in the realm of Sweden."

King Harald's face was lighted with a smile full of evil will. "These be tidings indeed," said he. "Take heed and rule thy speech, though for yonder in the high seat sitteth Styrbiorn the Strong, and I thought thou hadst known him, having thyself ere now fared a-cheaping in the Swede-realm."

The chapman's knees were loosened when he understood that this was Styrbiorn. And now were all men's eyes turned on Styrbiorn to see how he would take these news. Now so it was that at the first naming of his name by the chapman Styrbiorn waxed red to the ears and the roots of his hair. But when he heard of the crowning of Olaf the Lap-King he turned white with anger. He was leaned forth over the table on his elbows, with nostrils wide and in his eyes a light like as is in a lynx's eyes about to spring. He had in his right hand in that instant an ale-horn, and so mightily his hand shut on the horn that the horn cracked and burst under his hand-grip and the ale was wasted on the board. The chapman was afeared beholding him, and all men beheld him with some dread, for he seemed like to a man with the berserk-gang upon him, and well they deemed that that should be the bane of many a man there if Styrbiorn should break forth in that kind amongst them. So for a full minute's space not a man stirred nor spake in that hall, gazing all on Styrbiorn. Then, seeming to master himself, he spake and said, "When was this crowning?"

"Lord," answered the chapman, shaking and trembling, "they told me that was the third day after your going out from Upsala."

Styrbiorn smote down with a crash on the table the crushed ale-horn and threw back his head with a great laugh. Men thought there was naught good in the sound of that laughter. Then he drew from his arm a ring of gold, heavy and broad, and tossed it to Worm saying, "There's thanks for thy news of the Lap-King." Then he rose up and took by the hand Thyri, that was somewhat pale and shaken with these things. "Come, sweetheart," said he, "let's to bed. I must sail at daybreak for Jomsburg."

Styrbiorn busked him for the east next day at sunrise with nine ships. Ere he set forth he talked nigh an hour secretly with Biorn in Biorn's shut bed afore that men were astir. Biorn fared with him and Bessi Thorlakson. The rest of the host he set under the command of Bui the Thick, and bade them await his coming thither again to Alaburg, and that should be on the thirtieth day. King Harald noted these things. He was eager to know what Styrbiorn meant to do, but Styrbiorn would tell him nothing, only bidding him wait for him in Alaburg. "And what of Thyri?" said the King. "That thou shouldst sicken of her after a seven-nights' turtle-doving is a strange unheard of thing."

"Thyri saileth east with me," he answered.

"East to Jomsburg?" said the King. "Thou can'st

199

not bring thy wife into Jomsburg. There hath never been any woman brought thither."

"That concerneth not thee," said Styrbiorn.

The King was very ill content.

They went aboard now and sailed down the firth. But in Alaburg Harald the King abode ill at ease. Much he questioned Bui and Sigurd and the other lords of the Jomsburgers that were there, but found them but a dry well to draw from. And much he chafed to have sailed away out of the Limfirth with his following nor await Styrbiorn's return, or by what way soever to be rid of the Jomsburgers. But this seemed naught hopeful, but full of risk. So there he abode, chafing and discontented, and day by day the Dane-folk flocked to him in Alaburg according to the host-bidding he had made at Styrbiorn's behest up and down the land.

Styrbiorn came to Jomsburg about noon-tide the third day. When Palnatoki beheld Thyri there he took Styrbiorn apart and said, "What is this? She must go back. Thou knowest our law, that there shall be no woman brought into Jomsburg."

"There shall be now," said Styrbiorn. His eyes were fierce, and his speech stumbled more than of wont. "All things else that are mine I stake on this throw, to fare north now into Sweden and take it by force. But not her. Her I leave with you in Jomsburg to keep her safe for me. She is the Queen. She is the apple of mine eye, Palnatoki."

Palnatoki stood staring at him an instant with his eagle eyes; then, "This is a new turn," he said. "To Sweden?"

"I have heard tidings," said Styrbiorn. "Slow was I to raise war against King Eric. Until now he hath done me good. Thou knowest I abode quiet when the fates of ill luck sundered me and him, albeit he withheld from me my father's inheritance. I had rather let all go than bear war against him. But now hath he wrought me this shame and evil, to let crown a brat in my stead. And that is as much as to say I shall be cast out of my kingdom for ever. And that pat too, without thought or delay, while I near burst myself holding myself in. And now there is no help. It must be tried out now whether he or I be the stronger, and which of us must be King in Upsala."

Palnatoki took him by the hand. "I will do this for thee, Styrbiorn," he said. "And it is a thing I would not do for any other man, nor for myself neither. She shall come in. And now we must take rede for these greater matters."

In such wise was Queen Thyri taken into Jomsburg. Twenty-two days they abode there fitting out their ships and mustering the Wendland levies and others from those eastern parts which Styrbiorn had of late laid under him, till there were well nigh six score ships, both great ships and small, all manned and armed in Jomsburg harbour. At dawn of the twenty-third day they went ashipboard. It was a grey and misty morning, windless, with a drizzle of rain in the air. Styrbiorn came down to the ships with Palnatoki and Sigvaldi. Sigvaldi was to bide in Jomsburg as captain there. Palnatoki had been sick of a sickness these four or five days past, but there was no holding him from faring with Styrbiorn.

Styrbiorn had bound raven's wings on his helm. When Sigvaldi saw it, he said, "Some men would say thou wast fey, Styrbiorn, seeing thee commit so proud a blasphemy as bear raven's wings on thy helm. For this is a thing befitteth no man, nor yet the lesser Gods neither, but the All-Father alone. If thou wilt be counseled by me, leave them off. For well I think they shall bring us ill luck."

"They shall be taken off," answered he, "when they shall be hewn off in battle before Upsala. Or when I sit King there. No other way."

"I counsel thee," said Sigvaldi, "out of my love and loyalty. A man might say, to look on thee, thou hadst now clapt up thy good luck in a cage of gold. But I feared thee less in thy mad melancholy discontents last winter."

Styrbiorn laughed. "A doomed man's ice-hole," he said, "is never frozen. Have done with thy womanish fears."

But now befell this misfortune, that Palnatoki going aboard of his ship slipped foot and fell and brake his leg there. Men thought this a strange ill hap. Spite of

this, and his sickness yet heavy upon him, Palnatoki
would not be left behind; till in the end Styrbiorn got
his way with him, that he being unmeet for battle
should stay this while in Jomsburg and let Sigvaldi fare
in his stead with Styrbiorn into Sweden. There were
men that laid their heads together, seeing in this thing
an omen, and in the raven's wings. But most of them
trowed so much in their own might and main and in
Styrbiorn that they were in no mind to quiddle upon
such light matters as these. Sigvaldi held his peace,
and busked him without more ado to sail in Palnatoki's
stead. But men who knew him thought they knew that
his heart was not in that sailing.

Thyri came down with them to the ships. She was
brave and jolly of mien. But Biorn bethought him now
of her dream in Roiskeld two years since; and he thought
he knew she was finding it hard to put on so blithe a
face and press down her fears, seeing her lord now in
very earnest about faring North with a great host of
war.

They rowed out now from Jomsburg sea-gates in a
windless calm. Styrbiorn stood on the poop of his great
ship Ironbeak. She was both longer and taller of
build than the other ships, so that every man else in
that host must still be looking up at Styrbiorn and Styrbiorn down on them. Huge and dark was the spread
of the raven's wings above his head, fitter for a God
than for a mortal man. The mist thinned and broke,
and the sun looked over the land's edge and beamed full

on him with the fresh and clear brightness of morning.

Thyri stood there looking him farewell from the sea-wall of Jomsburg as the fleet steered west, and she was as a flower that is seen afar lonely on the sheer rock face of some wind-grieved mountain. The fog rolled up again and shut out Thyri and Jomsburg, leaving but a circle of sea about the ships and bright air and sunlight overhead. But as the ships passed out to sea under the outer headland they saw shadowy in the fog above them the shape of Moldi, gazing after them from the limit of the land.

So on the fourth day, being the thirtieth day appointed, came Styrbiorn back into the Dane-realm, and with him Sigvaldi and Biorn and other lords of the Jomsburgers, and they had five score and eleven ships of all sorts, fully manned. Near upon ten score ships of the Jomsburgers were already there in the Limfirth over against Alaburg, and some seven score of the King's ships.

Styrbiorn came aland and went to see Harald the King straightway. The King said, "Wilt thou bridge the Limfirth with thy ships, Styrbiorn?" Styrbiorn said he would have the King call a Thing now forthright in Alaburg. So the King let call a Thing, and when that was done then Styrbiorn let them know what was in his mind to do. "And now," he said, "I shall look for more than good words from you, father-in-law. There be here three hundred ships of us Jomsburgers ready to fare north with me. And I shall look to you for such furtherance as you may, both in men and ships."

"That," answered King Harald, "must give us a weighty cause to think upon. I seek no quarrel with the Swede-King. In west-viking we of the Dane-realm go our gate, whither we will. But that is an old saying, that the waves of the east sea do chant their songs to please the King of the Swedes."

"This is not the answer that will content me," said Styrbiorn.

The King said, "Thou hast still that trick, to fill thy purse with other men's fee." And he said, "Seeing thou art my son-in-law, for all I am not in this quarrel, we will yet lend you help of two score ships well found and manned."

"I must learn thee to leave thy niggishness," said Styrbiorn then. And this choice he gave them: either that they should fetch him two hundred ships, and that man withal whom he should choose to go with him, either else would Styrbiorn and his host sit down now in the land and dwellings of the Danes and eat up all their substance. "And that will seem a hard choice to you, and harder to bear. Yet shall you find the stronger must rule."

In the end, bethinking them that need giveth little choice, the King and his folk said yea to this. Styr-biorn said he would choose his man now to go with him, "And that shall be Harald the King." The King was mad wroth, but for none of his pleas nor offers would

Styrbiorn be moved. Styrbiorn was like a man who, with mind at ease now, sitteth with his hand on the helm steering with a fair wind toward his set resolve.

The fourth day after these things aforesaid Styrbiorn, with the whole great host of the Jomsburgers and the Danes, sailed for the north. King Harald would have fared aboard of his own ship, but Styrbiorn made him go with him in *Ironbeak*. The King had learnt now the wisdom of that saying, 'Never strive to match the sea,' and he would contend no more against Styrbiorn. Styrbiorn said to Biorn, "I will trust my father-in-law very discreetly. Till this fight be over, I will keep him by me like a doll. That will be good for him and good for his following. For they will guess well that if they keep not faith with me I will slay him out of hand."

So now they rowed out from the haven and down the Limfirth, and so set sail and hove out into the open sea. And first they steered south-eastward for the narrow seas betwixt Sealand and Skaney, meaning to coast so along Skaney-side and so north along the land toward Sigtun and Upsala. And that fleet needed wide sea-room to sail, as with foaming wake they stood out from the land, and it was long between the first ship and the last, and between that which steered outermost and that which steered nearest to landward.

But upon these things did the Danes that were left behind in Jutland sing this stave:

Ne'er would the Jute-folk
Yield gild to swift ships,
Till by the land stood
Sea-deer of Styrbiorn.
Now must the Dane-lord
· Follow that hosting:
Land-lorn and folk-lorn
Drees he his weird now.

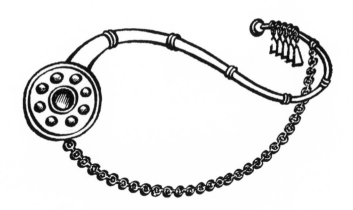

XIV

King Eric's Hosting

ERIC the King had espial since winter's end of all that was done in the south there. When news was brought him of the gathering to a head of that power in Jomsburg and the Dane-realm he took counsel first with Thorgnyr the Lawman. "And now," said the King, "is that need come upon us that we must lay our plans not as 'twere but Danes only and out-landers we must cope withal. For this, if it come about, shall bring into the land upon us a man of our own blood and line; and a man not to be driven alive out of the Swede-realm, I well think, once he shall have reached out hand to take it in my despite; and a man well loved of the folk too."

Thorgnyr looked and beheld awhile in silence the face of the King. Then, "Lord," he said, "there be two ways at every turning."

"I see but one," answered the King.

"That," said Thorgnyr, "is because you do hold your head so high that you may not of your greatness see this other way. And that is right, for it beseemeth not Kings to see all that groundlings can. Only, if you bid me counsel you in this, I must be no partial coun-seller. There be two ways."

"Stand or flee away?" said King Eric. "There is but one way for Kings."

Thorgnyr said, "You have answered me." And he

fell silent again. The King had turned his gaze away, and sat there leaning his chin heavily on one hand. Thorgnyr had liberty so to study the King's face, and it seemed to him the face of a man that hath put behind him both good and ill, and goeth in some deep resolve unto his fate. Thorgnyr pondered these things awhile. Then he said, "Now I shall not be slow to tell you my rede, Lord. And this it is: that you let call a Thing straightway in Upsala. There, what griefs soever the bonders have, right them out of hand, and better thus and thus the laws for the common sort and do men right, that men's hearts may incline mightily unto you. And therewithal let shear up the war-arrow, and call an all-folk hosting. And that were good rede, too, to stick the sea-ways that leadeth to Upsala, so as their ships may find no fair-way to come up at us through the Low."

They talked long on these things, and the King deemed good of Thorgnyr's redes and let do accordingly. And the King let hallow the holy Thing, and there was huge going together of the folk in the Thing-mead before Upsala, with the throng of the bonders and the common sort and the King's men and the following of the Earls and lords and landed men that were thither come at the King's bidding from all the lands and countries of the realm of Sweden. And thither were gathered Earl Aunund of Fiadrundarland and the Earls of Helsingland and Tenthland and East Gautland, Bodvar Auzurson of Leikberg with a great company,

Hermund the Old from Eyland, Koll Sigmundson of Acre-eres and Hiarrandi his brother, An the Black from Jarnberaland, Slaying-Starkad of Raening-oyce, Kalf Ongialdson of Kalmar, Steinfinn of Hising, Day Heriolfson and the lords of Jamtland and the Dales, Jorund of Vear, Liot Liotson of the Knolls, Oliver Leatherneck of Dalby, and many more. And earliest come of all the great men was Skogul-Tosti, the father of Sigrid the Queen. For in that same hour when the King's bidding reached Tosti he took horse and rode from Arland, two days and a night without sleep or stay, till he was come into Upsala.

Men were all agog now with tidings likely and unlikely of Styrbiorn's farings: one saying that he was already come aland beside Mirkwood and had burnt up the whole wood with fire: another that he was gotten into Norway and had slain Earl Hakon there in a pitched battle, and would shortly fare over the Keel into Sweden; another that he was turned away east for Garthrealm with all his ships, and all danger past: another that they were shut up in Jomsburg by the Wends: another that he was dead: another that he and the King were friends again, and that he was even now secretly in the King's house in Upsala. With all which busy and contrary talk was the whole Thing in an hubbub. Nor was it clear how much men were like to hold by the King and follow him when it should come to fighting, and how much their minds inclined to Styrbiorn. But when the King spake to them of that which he was

minded to do for the bettering of the laws and right-
ing of the wrongs of men, according to the wholesome redes of Thorgnyr, then were they that had been
eager before to do him service yet the more eager when
they heard him say those words, and went all together
praising the King and shouting that he should lead them
into battle; and they that were of the other party held
their peace or changed their minds.

And now the King let proclaim an all-folk hosting.

The fifth night after, King Eric and his men being
served and set to the supper, came a man of his with
sure tidings from the south that Styrbiorn, with so great
an host of war-ships as had not been seen together till
that day by living man, was sailed out of the Limfirth
and thence along Skaney-side for Sweden. The King
had not yet fully eaten, that there came into the hall a
man of his bodyguard to let the King know that hither
was come Earl Wolf, Styrbiorn's foster-father and
mother's brother, ridden up to the King's garth dirtied
up to the horse's belly, "And would fain have speech
with you, Lord, but durst not trust himself unto you
but and if you will handsel him peace and safety."

"There is little need of that," said the King. "When
hath he known me to be sly, quaint and false, were it my
very foe in mine hand to do of him as I will? But this
is my friend and kinsman. Tell him he shall have
peace."

When Earl Wolf was come into the hall and stood

before King Eric, the King said, "Thou rodest not hither to the Thing. A poor man that is true is better than an Earl if he be false."

"That I am come to you now, King," answered the Earl, "let that speak for my truth. And never was greater need of good will 'twixt kinsman and kinsman. And 'tis that hath brought me, 'gainst all wise fears and mine own good."

"Thou look'st afeared," said the King. "Yet I have known thee for a brave man."

"I fear not for myself," answered he, "but for you, King; and for others."

"Hath Styrbiorn sent thee to me?" asked the King.

"No," he said. "I'll walk in no nets, thinking I am hid. He hath not sent me. Yet I think he'll welcome me with both hands if you will send me to him."

"Hast had speech of him?"

The Earl said, "Yes."

"Is he landed?"

"King," answered the Earl, "he is landed Southway by Mirkwood. Late yester-evening."

"Alone?" asked the King.

"With an host not to be dealt with in battle," said the Earl. "There is little time left: you see me ridden hot haste to you: I have killed two horses under me——"

"Why?" said the King. "To lend me aid against him?"

Looking in the King's countenance that seemed hard

and ice-cold, and hearing the accent of his speech, inhospitable and passionless as the voice of the sea grinding on a shingle beach, the Earl winced, as a man might wince under a wintry blast. "I came to you, King," he said, "to make peace while there is yet time."

"He hath come aland," said the King. "Time is gone by, then. I said that if ever he should come again into the Swede-realm, that should be his death."

"Say not so, King," said Earl Wolf, and his face was ashen-hued. "Is all your old memories worn so out of mind? Because you are like and like, do not for that sake break one another. You would not hear him, but did send him into this woeful banishment unheard. That which befell on that ill night——"

"Hold," said the King, breaking in upon him. "Dost thou not know that the man who speaketh of that night in my hearing shall lose nothing but his life? And my peace which I sware unto thee shieldeth thee not as for that."

The Earl bowed his head. "For your old love sake and kinship, Lord, will you not bend, and it were but one finger's breadth? For so meseemeth, even so little a thing might set all a-right: even if you should but take back the whole kingdom into your own hand, and let him then be heir unto you. Even should you still hold by your great rigour against him, to ban him from the land all your lifedays, yet I think I should persuade his mind, fierce and masterful though he be, to swallow it. Though you should live (and that is to be

hoped for) unto a deep old age, yet is it to be looked for
that he should live longer than you, King, being he is
now so young and you thrice his years: then might he
take after you in Upsala; but now you have broken all
his hope and done him the worst wrong, and that remedi-
less, to crown your own young son to be King with
you in his stead. Will you not undo this deed? And
then, on my head be it if I send him not away again
out of Sweden. I'll ride all night to bring him the
news."

Earl Wolf ended so, and stood waiting on the King's
answer. The King, that had harkened to all this with
clouded brow and downward look, and with hands
pressed open, palms downward, on the board before
him, lifted his face now and gazed steadily in the Earl's
face. "Whet me or let me," he said: the harm is done.
Much could I forbear and much treat on with a man
of mine own blood, and hard it must go with me now
to say nay to this. Yet so it must be. The man that
hath once drawn sword against me, with him I will make
no atonement. It must now be tried out whether of us
twain must be King in Upsala."

There was that in the King's face, and in the hard
and chilling command that was in his voice, that took
all heart out of the Earl for further speech. For a
minute he stood looking on the King: then he turned
his gaze right and left about the shadowy hall, meeting but looks that were borrowed from the King's, grim
and set; save only that old man Thorgnyr, whose coun-

tenance none might read: Helgi and Thorir and Thorgisl with sneering looks and the swagger of court bravery: and last, the Queen's lovely face with eyes dark and doubtful and with nostrils dilated a little, like some fierce and graceful beast's at the scent of blood.

"Wilt thou stay with me, Earl, or go back to him?" said the King.

"Is it in my choice, Lord?"

"It is in thy choice," said the King. "And if thou choosest to go, I will send thee with safe conduct. For like enow the ways will be little safe for one faring southward from Upsala, sith I have bid out a war-gathering with an arrow-bidding. And thou art not a man unknown to folk, nor is thy kindred unknown and ties of friendship."

"This will ever be said of you, Lord," said Earl Wolf then, "that you are of all kings the most open-handed and the most high-minded. But that you are too hard-hearted and stubborn of bent, it hath been seen to-night. And this may be the beginning of woe to many."

Earl Wolf took leave of the King now and rode south again, heavy of heart, to Styrbiorn his foster-son. But in Upsala was all gotten ready for battle. By then were the stakes stuck in the fair-way below Sigtun, and weapons and war-gear dealt out among the bonders, and the fighting men marshalled under their captains and lords so as each man should know his place and what to do when the time should come. But with such un-looked-for sudden speed had Styrbiorn fared north from Denmark, that the King wanted yet nigh the third part of his host he had looked to muster, and hour by hour from the south came men with tidings of Styrbiorn's approach. And it was clear now that the King must fight with that force he had, for little likelihood there was that he should be able to hold off the battle long time enough for all his folk to gather under his banners.

In all this making ready had the King chiefest part, and men marked in what unwearying way he wrought, yet like a man that is without gladness in his task and without thought for the morrow; and he fared through the army and took counsel and issued his commands as a smith might smithy or a digger delve a ditch, so that men thought the heart was gone from him, and but his strength and wisdom only and his iron purpose yet living in him and ruling these things.

Sigrid the Queen came to Thorgnyr and said, "Thou mayst say this is not women's work, but 'tis this now lieth us on hand, to hold the realm against Styrbiorn until our full host be gathered. And as things stand now, if he should avail to bring his host upon us and force the King to battle ere he be ready, like enough we were all shent."

"That is true," said Thorgnyr.

"Hast thou thought on this," said the Queen: "to gather together all the beasts of draught, both horses and oxen, that you may, and bind pikes and bills upon them so as they shall stick forth from the beasts, and let thrallfolk and ill-doers be driven before you to drive on the beasts against Styrbiorn and his folk? That should fetch him mickle man-spill in the first brunt, and small loss to us, and should even the odds somewhat. Or what thinkest thou?"

"Some would think it an ill deed," said Thorgnyr.

"If thou deemest hopefully of it," said she, "I would have thee lay it before the King as thine own rede. He will not take aught from me. Moreover, I would not that he should know that 'twas I thought on't."

The same hour Thorgnyr laid this before the King. The King listened without changing countenance and was silent awhile, as if weighing the matter. Then his look darkened and he said, "Many will blame me for this and say 'tis a poor game to play. But is it not all a poor game, Thorgnyr, that I have set mine hand to: to bear war against myself? Yet will I play it out, and leave naught untried: no, not this nor a worse thing, if thou canst find it. Let set about it straight."

When Queen Sigrid knew that this rede of hers was taken by the King she was glad at heart. She let send for Helgi and charged him saying, "I will have thee do this, Helgi: thou shalt seek out that little hairy ox that Styrbiorn set so much store by, and so bring it about that he shall be arrayed in the midst and front of all the baggage-beasts. That will be good sport, that they should meet the last time in battle indeed, 'stead of as heretofore in make-believe."

Helgi promised this, to do as the Queen bade him. But it came not about, for Moldi was now in Jomsburg.

Now was it the third evening since tidings were first brought to King Eric in Upsala of Styrbiorn's coming aland at Mirkwood. And now was all ready to the King's hand and his army weaponed and marshalled and the beasts furnished and their drivers held in readiness. And on this had he determined, to give Styrbiorn battle in the ings and meadows on the left bank of Fyriswater a few miles below Upsala. Nor did the King lack aught save only men; but that was a sore lack, and might, if it so fell out, danger his whole state and kingdom. But there were fresh forces that should swell the King's army, some coming in hourly and others due on the morrow or the morrow's morrow.

All that day had the King busied himself with the army, looking to every point, even to the weapons and gear of the meanest man of the host and the cooking gear and meat and drink, that every man might be well fed and in frame for the fight; and he spake with men and heartened them and bade them quit themselves well when it should come to the proof. And now, when all was to his mind, he with his bodyguard rode at evening with Thorgnyr down to the head of the firth at River-oyce, mainly to ease his mind with

riding after the long day's toil, but with this intent
also, to see for sure that Styrbiorn's fleet had not sailed
up into the firth despite the sticking of the channel at
Sigtun. For if that should befall, then might they
come upon the King's forces and Upsala from all another side than that whence they were looked for.

Day was fading as the King and Thorgnyr rode
down to the desolate shore at the firth-head. The wind
blew a gale from the west. The first was empty: not
a ship nor a boat: only iron clouds, murky and unbroken,
that tore out of the western airt and passed overhead
and away endlessly down the dark eastern sky behind
the wind-swept pinewoods. Eric the King sat silent
on his horse there, looking through half-shut eyelids
up-wind as if into the heart or quickening womb of
that turmoil. Thorgnyr sat silent beside him: neither
he nor any man that was there durst speak word to the
King, for he seemed fallen in a mood that brooks not
speech. After a time the King, troubled perhaps by
his horse's fidgetting, dismounted, tossed his reins to a
house-carle of his, and walked down a few paces to the
edge of the low cliff that overhung the stony beach
where the waves broke and thundered. There he stood
alone. Night shut down. There was no moon, and
sea and sky were now mingled and blurred together;
and, to a man so striving to gaze up that baffling and
hurtling wind, there was naught to be seen save row
after row of breakers bodied in unending succession out
of the womb of night, and livid white in the windy

darkness. One after another broke into foam, first along but a short strip of wave, then spreading quickly its foaming crest left and right. And in that blackness, where land-mark and sea-mark were swallowed up, that spreading gave the appearance of white things first seen afar then rushing shoreward with a speed that seemed terrible and beyond nature, broad-side on the flood.

A full hour the King stood watching them rush out of the remote dark to their ruin on the shore, by tens and by hundreds, and naught left but the black back-wash at his feet. Then, without a word, he turned about, took horse again, and rode with his company back through the night to Upsala.

XV

Fyrisfield

STYRBIORN lay with his host two days' march north of Mirkwood that night that Earl Wolf his foster-father came back from the north. The sentinels knew the Earl and brought him in through the camp. It was the deep and dead time of the night. The waning moon, scarce three hours risen, shone bright in a serene heaven that was without cloud save for a slanting band of mackerel sky down in the southwest, and the bigger stars that were not put out by the strong moonshine blinked and sparkled. There was rime on the grass, so that it crunched under their tread. As they came past the horse-lines, there was here and there the sound of a horse kicking or stamping: a long way off at the far end of the lines a torch showed red, where a man was changing the tethers to make his horse comfortable: the tap of his mallet sounded dead on the stillness. On every side, as far as the eye might reach, the low skin tents lay mushroom-like in the stark white and black of the moonlight.

The Earl looked now and then at the faces of the men that guided him, and their faces seemed white and wooden, so that hard it was to know them for men of right flesh and blood; and like to them seemed the faces of all other waking men they encountered, of other sentinels as they came through that sleeping camp. Everywhere the Earl heard, as he picked his way among the tents, little noises of sleep, of sleeping men breathing heavily, turning and grunting. And here and there were men asleep in the open, their heads and shoulders muffled in cloaks, and they slept in awkward shapes and looked dead and piteous. Their snores and uneasy sighings came ghostly on the vast emptiness of the night, and the peace of it, and the stillness, and the cold of the quiet moon.

They brought in the Earl now to the mid part of the camp where Styrbiorn slept; and there was there a great fire burning, and Styrbiorn slept in his cloak beside the fire, for he loved not tents, and the men of his bodyguard were asleep there round about him. There was a house-carle of his named Thorhall kept guard at that hour. He greeted the Earl and asked him if he brought any tidings. The Earl said he would tell that to Styrbiorn. "If you bring peace," said Thorhall, "tell him now. But if it is as we think likely, then that will be better to let him sleep his sleep out."

The Earl stood silent a minute, looking down on Styrbiorn, and the sleeping face of him was tranquil as a man's that is cast in his first sleep beside his bride. And that seemed wondrous in him that slept there on the cold ground in a camp of war, on the eve of doings that he was well minded should break either himself or all the rest of the North.

"Let it wait till morning," said the Earl.

. . . .

228

When the morrow dawned and men were astir again, the Earl came to Styrbiorn and told him all. Styrbiorn said, "I could have saved thee thy journey, foster-father."

The Earl paused. Then he said, "Wilt thou not turn back, even now?"

Styrbiorn shook his head. "No," he answered.

Styrbiorn bade strike camp now. He brought his army by great journeys all that day and the next, north through the woods and uplands till they came at even of the next day down to the flats of Fyrisfield below Upsala, and there lay the King his uncle with a very great host. Styrbiorn took a stand now and stayed his army in the open meadow-land over against the King. And so great were the armies of Styrbiorn and of the King that no man that was there had ever seen so great a war-gathering in all the Northlands. They deemed it over-late in the day to join battle, and both hosts camped there on the field.

Now when it was high day men busked them for war, and Styrbiorn let cast his host into battle array and set up the banners, and his captains and lords of the Jomsburgers gave out the word and bade their men take heed to their places whereas each man was marshalled. Styrbiorn set up his banner and there were the men of his bodyguard arrayed, Bessi and Gunnstein and Ere-Skeggi to wit and Valdimar of Holmgarth and many more with their messmates and house-

carles; and Biorn the Broadwickers' Champion was
there, for he was minded that in this fight as in others
aforetime he should be not afar from Styrbiorn. There
were also in the mid battle those Swedes that had taken
Styrbiorn's side at his landing, and over these was Earl
Wolf now set in command. But on the right hand
from the main battle was the battle of Bui, and there
fared along with him Sigurd Cape his brother and a
great host of the Jomsburgers and the Wendish levies
and others from the east. And on the left had those
sons of Strut-Harald place, Heming and Thorkell the
High, lacking their eldest brother: for Sigvaldi had
sneaked away under the cloak of darkness on Skaney-
side. Yet was there not the tenth part even of his
own men would go with him, but bade him go to the
devil and went all under Heming and Thorkell. And
that made great wonder, for Sigvaldi was commonly
a man well followed and obeyed. And on the left
went also the Danes, King Harald Gormson's following, and their captains were Ivar of Weatherisle and
Hiort the son of Sighvat and Einar the Red. But
King Harald himself Styrbiorn would not suffer to depart from under his own hand, so that he went willy-
nilly in the mid battle with Styrbiorn. Styrbiorn let
make a shield-burg about King Harald.

Styrbiorn now said to Biorn his foster-brother, "I
was never a talker, and now thou must talk to them for
me: and say thus and thus." And therewith he taught
Biorn, in his ear, with swift stuttering speech, what he

should say. And Biorn, standing forth beside Styrbiorn in the face of that great army, spake to them and
said: "Thus saith Styrbiorn the Strong, and for that
he is a man of deeds more than a man of talk, he
charged me say it unto you; and thus saith Styrbiorn:
'I have this to say, that I shall not flee from this battle.
I shall either have the victory here'over King Eric, or I
shall fall here else. So that if it be my fate to over-
live this battle, then will it lie in my hand to do you
good; for in my hand will lie then all the lands and
fee that be in the realm of Sweden, to deal them out
unto them that deserved well of me. And now, the
swiftlier we fall upon them the better hope have we of
victory, for delay fighteth of their side. For so long
as King Eric shall stand yet in the field against us, those
that yet flock to Upsala to his host-bidding will follow
him and strengthen him with fresh folk when we shall
have foughten unto weariness; but if we put him to a
rout now, then will they go quietly under our hand and
submit them to me. So now let us make the brunt so
hard that they turn aback that are foremost of them, and
then will each fall across the other.' "

There was not a man in that army that lost a word
of this, hearing indeed the voice of Biorn but gazing
the while on their lord out of whose shadow he spoke:
on the great stature of Styrbiorn towering above them,
and on the great raven-wings shadowing like death. As
Biorn ended, Styrbiorn reared his head yet higher and
shouted in a great voice. "Your watch-word for egg-

ing on one another to battle: Forth, forth, Styrbiorn's
men!"

Therewith came the captains with their companies
and went forth before the banners and let blow the war-
blast and cried out, "Forth, forth, Styrbiorn's men!"
And the whole host set up the war-shout and set on
against the array of King Eric, shooting with arrows
and twirl-spears and stones and hand-axes and shaft-
flints. But ere they were come up and at hands with the
enemy, the King's ranks opened and let forth against
them the beasts of burden armed as aforesaid; and these
were now driven on by a great company of thralls and
ill-doers that were themselves pricked from behind
with spears and bills, and fire was set now among the
tails of the horses and oxen so that in a moment they
were all run wild with the terror and scathe of the
fire, and stampeded all in a body against Styrbiorn's host.
And now was an evil din of cattle bellowing and horses
squealing, and there was many a man slain there or
trampled or maimed or limb-lopped and their array near
broken, and much folk fell both of the Jomsburgers and
of them that drave on the beasts; but the King's fighting men held aback all the while on the skirts of this
tumult, and few of them took hurt there, but they held
well their line waiting their time for an onslaught.
But Styrbiorn's host, besides the wounding and man-
slaying that there befell them, must spend strength on
butchers' work and the hewing down of naked thralls,
while their enemies abode fresh waiting on their time.

As soon as this first brunt, wherein the baggage animals bare chiefest part, died down a little, and the beasts
and the thrall-folk were slain or driven away, the King's
folk plunged down upon the battle of the Jomsburgers
and gave them so hard an onfall that well nigh was
their whole army put to a rout now. And now was
Styrbiorn's line bent back, and man hewed man, and
hard and woundsome went the battle until past noon-
day. And as the day wore it was well seen what great
good the King had won by his taking to Queen Sigrid's
reed of the baggage animals, for his men were un-
wearied yet and full of all eagerness and fain of
weapon-play, while their foes, for all their great hardi-
ness and long use of wars and battles, were near overcome with very weariness. Withal, whensoever there
fell a man on Styrbiorn's side there was none to take his
place; but all day long were the King's losses made
good by new forces that would still be coming by tens
and twenties: late stragglers to his host-bidding, yet
welcomer now an hundredfold than had they come in
two days since.

Yet for all their weariness and the odds against them
the men of Jomsburg blenched nowise nor slacked not
from the fight. Styrbiorn fared all day through the
battle where the work was briskest, and the raven's
wings that he bare aloft on his helm became a lode-star
unto his own men and unto his enemies a sign of dule
and undoing. Men thought he fared that day like one
shielded by some God, or like a wizard whom iron will

,bite not: so little he warded himself from blow or thrust,
'yet took never a wound. But of many men he took the
life there, and these of greatest note: Earl Aunund,
namely, and Kalf of Kalmar and Karl Heriolfson that
was sister's son to old Thorgnyr and held for a great
champion.

Eric the King had his bodyguard about him, and they
made a shield-burg about the King. Helgi was captain
of the King's bodyguard. Twice and thrice Styrbiorn
came nigh to them, and it seemed to them as if he was
minded to break the shield-burg: but each time he turned
aside and bare not weapon against the shield-burg nor
against the King. But now, as evening drew on and
with all his force of numbers the King yet found that
he might not bear back the Jomsburgers a step, but barely
held them, and Styrbiorn fought yet like flaming fire,
the King sent forth his berserks, An the Black and his
kinsmen, six in company against Styrbiorn, if haply they
might overcome him faring all together against him and
haply so make an end.

Biorn saw them as they came a-thrusting through the
press of the battle. He shouted to Styrbiorn, who bestrode in that instant Valdimar of Holmgarth that was
fallen with a spear-thrust through the thigh and two
foemen making to slay him, but Styrbiorn beat them
back and shouted to his men to succour Valdimar. And
in this instant while Styrbiorn had his hands full with
those twain, came An against him six in company, and
they set on him from both sides. An was a man both

big and strong. He was swart of hue, and the black
hair of him was so long that he tucked it under his
belt behind. He and his fellows had now the berserk-
gang upon them: their bellowing was like the bellowing
of the hell-dead out of hell, and their mouths slavered
as they rushed to the onset, and they bit on their shield-
rims, and their eyes flamed like the eyes of a cat-a-
mountain. That was Gizur Arnliotson, An's young-
est brother, that leapt first at Styrbiorn, out-running his
fellows, and thrust at his belly with his spear, a two-
handed up-heaving thrust as of a man tossing hay.
Styrbiorn leapt sideways high in the air, so that the
stroke missed, and, as he came to earth again, he crashed
down the heavy iron rim of his shield into An's face,
that was come up now beside him on the left and was
minded to have smitten Styrbiorn with a great mowing
sweep of his long and heavy sword. So mightily Styrbiorn drave down the shield rim that it sheared through
the nose-guard and clave the face and drave out the gag-
teeth and brake all his jaws in pieces, and An fell down
and was dead on the instant. With the same motion
Styrbiorn swung his great double-headed axe against
Gizur that was louted forward with the force of his
spent spear-stroke. Styrbiorn's axe crashed down
through the collar-bone and brake in all the bones of his
back, so that the blood of him was splashed in the air
like the spray of a breaking wave. That was Gizur's
bane-sore. In the meanwhile had Biorn slain another
of those berserks with his spear, but he thrust it so hard

into the man's head behind the ear that the blade was jammed in the bones of the head, like an axe in an oak-tree stump, and the spear snapped off at the socket. And therewith, ere Biorn might draw sword, set on another of the berserks against him; but Styrbiorn, seeing that, hewed at the man with his axe, and the axe cut through the man's byrny and split his belly like a herring from the belt down, so that his bowels fell out. Now had Biorn gotten his sword drawn. So ended that bout that there fell there An the Black and his five fellows. Styrbiorn took never a wound, but Biorn gat a flesh-wound in the chin.

Now it began to be dark, so that men might not tell friend from foe. Men saw now that neither side might claim victory as for that day's battle, and so battle-worn were they for the most part of either side that scarce might they bear weapon aloft. So they blew to a truce now and fared back to their camps.

Eric the King slept that night with his army. But he sent men back with tidings to Upsala to let them know the battle was not yet foughten out, but all well. He kenned his host and found that he had gotten much man-spilling, yet he thought he knew that Styrbiorn must have gotten as much and more. His folk were in good heart when they went to rest, albeit against all their expectations that long day's fighting had not ended the thing. For news came in about supper-time that Skogul-Tosti, whom the King had sent north for fresh levies out of Helsingland, was nigh at hand now with a good force of men. Too late they were for that day's battle, but they came in about the middle night, and the King misdoubted not but that with those fresh forces he should on the morrow have the victory. For Styrbiorn could look for no fresh forces to make good his losses.

Queen Sigrid the Haughty, waiting in Upsala, liked ill of these delays. There was great thronging of folk in Upsala, women for the most part and children and old men; and all day long came tidings dribbling in, to cast them now into untimely gladness now again into dread; and all day long, as wounded men came with tidings of this man's deeds or of that man's slaying, was the noise of women mourning. The Queen was tired of all this by even-tide. When they told her that the King would come not home that night but there must yet be battle again on the morrow, she smiled scornfully but said never a word.

The next day after were the like comings and goings in Upsala and the like suspense. And they that had looked for easy victory found soon enough there was like to be no such thing. Until afternoon there had been naught to see of the battle from near Upsala, for their fighting was all in the wide and open lower part of the vale, that was shut off from view by the steep slopes of Windbergsfell that stood on the left to one look-ing south down the river. The crest of the fell rose in cliffs of rock, red and rotten, and the loose scree lay on the fell-side like a trailing garment, covering all the slope down from the cliff-wall to the level flats below. But now the battle was come north into the higher stretch of the valley betwixt the fell and the river, and the Queen went forth and came to King Olaf's howe, if haply she might avail from that point of vantage to descry somewhat of their doings in the ings of Fyris-water. She climbed the howe and stood there gazing southaway, even as she had gazed four years ago when she had stood there and looked on Styrbiorn trying his strength with Moldi. "I saw fetches then," she said in herself: "I saw him as if read and battle-slain in the mead yonder. And I thought not this day should come when such a sight should be meat and drink to me."

Her women that had followed her out from the King's house huddled about her on the howe, all a-flutter with the uncertain dread of that day and the great issues of it. But Sigrid stood above them stately as a birch tree of the hills. She was muffled to the chin in a cloak of green silk broidered with gold and collared and purfled with minivere. That red cloak which she had a year ago put off for Styrbiorn she had burnt next morning. The hood of her cloak was fallen backward, baring the flame-like splendour of her hair above the smooth brow and stately and lovely face of her. There was in her face, as she gazed south with haughty lip and level chin, so much beauty as the Gods might throw up hands and strive no more to better it

were they to frame the world anew; and so much gentle-
ness and womanish pity and softness as a man shall find
in the rain-cold rock of the sea. Two miles and more
down from Upsala the battle swayed and weltered, in
its large mass, clear to see from that place of prospect.
And even as the sun wheeling westward in that cloud-
less sky lengthened the shadows bit by bit, so and with
such-like even and unrelenting motion was the battle
rolled north. Until, as evening neared, the Queen
watching from Olaf's howe could discern amid that
surge and coil of war a man here and a man there
stand out clear to view; and now she saw ever and
again, riding the battle as an eagle rides upon the storm,
the black wings of Styrbiorn's helm. And always
where those wings flew, there swung back the battle-
tide before them, ebbing terribly backward towards
Upsala. And the south wind carried the roar of it
north over those water-meadows like the roar of a
sea.

The Queen watched from the howe there till dusk.
Her women were crouched about her like frightened
sheep, speechless, clinging one to another, sobbing for
fear and their teeth chattering. She, heedless of their
presence this hour gone by, turned now and with a sharp
and imperious word bade them gather their wits and
follow her home.

Lamps were lighting as the Queen came into the
King's garth. At every hand were wounded men,
within door and without. Helgi was there in the door,

harnessed as from battle, as the Queen came in. She
halted to greet him and ask for tidings.

"There must be one day more," answered he.

"What of the King?" she asked.

"All safe and sound," said Helgi.

The voice of him sounded strange, and she peered at
him through the uncertain light in the porch there of
twilight and the reflection of the lamps within-door.
She saw he was propped against the door-jamb.

"And what of that other?"

"Not all I'd wish," answered Helgi. "He hath come
too near me, though I fetched him a sword-stroke o' the
huckle-bone may well last him for a keepsake." He
laughed, and his legs gave way beneath him. The
Queen caught him in her arms. Blood gushed from his
mouth. She heard him say in a choking voice, "A hath
paid me, Queen."

They bare Helgi into the King's hall. He was dead
ere night was done. Hour after hour long after night-
fall came wounded men back to Upsala, some to be
leeched and some to die. No man came back that
night who might stand on his feet and hold spear or
sword; for things were come to this pass that, for all
his strength of men and the succours that Tosti had
brought him, the King was worsted in that day's battle.
His folk had with all their might and daring but barely
availed to hold off Styrbiorn from Upsala, in so much
that had there been but another hour of daylight it was

like enough there had been an end, and the King's whole army broken and done away.

The King abode with his army. They had no time to take their tents and camp-gear with them as they gave back fighting step by step. So the women-folk and the old men brought meat and drink down to them on Fyrisfield at night-time, and they lay out night-long under their shields.

Styrbiorn and his host had use that night of the King's baggage and war-booths. Styrbiorn had a wound from his fighting with Helgi, and there was not one of those lords of Jomsburg but had taken some hurt that day. Battle-weary they were, yet high of mettle and with hearts at ease, they and every man of their army, as they sat down for that second night in the highways of the battle. For they had fought at the beginning against heavy odds and had evened them at length, and the advantage of the day was theirs, only night parted them.

Earl Wolf came to Styrbiorn where he sat after supper nigh to a great fire, and about him sat the lords of the Jomsburgers and men of his bodyguard. "That will be well for us, kinsman," said the Earl, "ere men turn them to sleep, if thou shouldst make prayer now unto the Gods that they shape things to-morrow as we would have it, and help us, not our enemies."

"I will do that, foster-father," answered he. "Yet

is it in our own might and main that I would have us
put our trust. I had liever thank the Gods when we
shall have won the day than go a-praying to them be-
forehand."

But all deemed that good, if Styrbiorn should pray to
the Gods. So Styrbiorn did on his great iron helm
winged with raven's wings, and took in hand his great
naked sword of shining iron, and so stood up in the
smoky glare. And he shouted unto Thor, calling upon
his name and saying, "Do that I to-morrow have victory!" The voice of him so shouting was like the
thunder of a battle-horn. From wing to wing of the
camp men heard and knew his voice, and they shouted
likewise unto Thor from fire to fire. Men heard in
the King's camp that shouting, and even in Upsala.
Little comfort they took hearing it.

About the middle night King Eric rose up and waked
two or three of his bodyguard, bidding them go with
him. The King took helm and shield and spear and
fared now through the black night to Upsala and came
to the temple. He bade his men bring torches and
wait in the outer court of the temple, while he himself went in to the inner shrine where was the altar and
holy place of Odin, and the ring and the twigs and
the blood-bowls. It was black darkness there, made
visible by the faint and fitful beams of the torches without. The King laid hand upon the ring and prayed.
Nigh an hour he stood there a-praying, and he sware

oath unto the All-Father that if He should vouchsafe
to him victory in this battle, then would he after ten
years give himself unto Odin. And the King prayed,
and made new his oath, and looked for a sign. But
there was naught but the blackness and the silence and
the smell of blood, and from without the moan of
women that wailed their dead, sleepless and uncomforted
through all the bitter night. Then the King made an
end of his prayers, and came again to his camp and
fell on sleep until the morning.

Now began the third day of that battle. All the
morning was the same tale to tell of every wounded
man that found his way back, of hard fighting and the
King's men hard put to it, and no sight of the end yet.
Things seemed to be worse as the hours went by, and
the news worse and less hopeful that the wounded
brought. But in the afternoon it was not that the news
was worser but that the stream of it dried up. They
that now came in from the fight had the look of men
who know well that it is done of them. They would
say naught but this only: that there was battle yet
sharper than on either of the former days, and the
King's folk beaten back step by step, yet holding together.

The day was now three parts done, and Queen Sigrid
sat with her women in her bower the windows whereof
looked south out of Upsala. Till afternoon she had
beheld the battle from Olaf's howe; then, as if angry

in her proud heart at the long uncertainty of that which she had no might to sway nor hasten, she came within doors again and sat there silent and waiting. But no end came: naught save that ceaseless sea-sound only of this third day's fighting, flooding now nigh to the outer fields and home-meads of Upsala.

On a sudden, as, lost in her brooding, the Queen rested her gaze on the steep crest of Windbergsfell that showed on the left, a mile away belike, sharp against the sky, it was as if smoke came all along the edge of the fell, and in the next instant came a rumble as of thunder, drowning the dull growl of the battle. The Queen stood up. The hill's edge was all hidden now with a dirty brown smoke-pall. The muttering rose to a roar, pulsing and pausing and swelling again. It seemed to them there as if the very timbers of the house were shaken. One of her women screamed and cried out that here was the world's end come upon them and the beginning of Ragnarok. The child Olaf ran to his mother's skirt. Sigrid abode erect and unmoved, but her face was white as death. There seemed to be now a strange and evil silence. Then the old steady battle-rumour began again. Yet not so steady now. Little by little it seemed to die down again, as if the battle were rolled away, or as if so many were slain now that they that yet lived availed not to hold up that battle-din. That cloud that hung on the fell's brow thinned and lightened.

The Queen went out into the garth, and so out and

on to Upsala brink. Folk were thronging there, one saying one thing and one saying another. None knew what was befallen. One man said that the main fell was overset and fallen down upon the King's army and Styrbiorn's. There was fog in the air over Fyrisfield, and it hung thickest on the skirts of the fell to the eastward. There was naught to see. The Queen came again to her bower and sat in her chair there. She had taken a sword from the bottom of a chest she had by her, and she sat with the sword unsheathed and across her knees. Her women asked her what she meant to do with that sword. She drew back her lips and smiled. "That question showeth little wit. Do you think I will be taken living by Styrbiorn?"

At sundown came that old man Thorgnyr riding into the King's garth. They brought him in to the Queen where she sat waiting. "Speak quickly," she said. "There is not a man come hither since that befell, and I know nothing. Must it be to-morrow too?"

Thorgnyr said, "It is ended."

The Queen caught her breath.

"Have no fear," he said. "True it is that we were almost clean done; but in the nick of time to save us befell so great a wonder as you must have seen and heard, Queen, that the scree burst up on the fell, and that came all adown upon the host of Styrbiorn and slew him a great part of his folk, but our own folk being away from the mountain took no hurt. And in the dust and pother of it, this good thing befell too, that the Dane-King (whom he had kept beside him until now) took rede to escape away, and galloped a-horseback over to his own people on their left beside the river, and made them give over and come out from the battle and flee away. So were the rest taken now by our folk both in front and in flank, and not yet free from the scree-fall. And now of his army is almost nothing left than a shadow thereof. And it is finished now, all save the pursuit and slaying."

"What of him?" said the Queen. "What of Styrbiorn?"

"The last I saw of him," answered Thorgnyr, "he with a score were stood together back to back on a knoll of grass in the midst o' the field there. They had stricken down their standard-shafts into the earth, and our folk were closing on them from all sides."

"Did he yet bear aloft those black wings?" said she.

"Yes," he answered.

The Queen abode motionless. She said nothing for a minute. Then she spoke again: "Why didst thou not wait to see it out?"

"There was no need," he answered. "It could end but one way. I am an old man, and it is not to be wondered at if I am tired."

She looked at him silent a moment with her lips parted. Then, "But one way for him," she said: "that is true. Yet, I would know."

Thorgnyr said nothing. The Queen stepped for-

ward and he made way for her. She muffled her cloak
about her and walked with swift sure steps across the
garth and out into the open field. The light was fading now. All the low sky south-westward was filled
with a long bank of grey and shapeless cloud. There
was a window of a cold buff-colour far down over the
river, and higher up a great streak of a deep dark blood-
red that looked strange and ill-boding amid those dull
and lifeless hues. There was fallen a dead silence
now on those meadows. The dust-fog was gone, but
night-mists began to roll up from the river. The
Queen waited there in the gathering dusk. Her eyes
were bright. As men passed her by, coming by twos
and threes back from the field, they saluted her,
marking her proud and triumphant bearing. Night
closed in, and yet the King came not. She went in
now.

Eric stood on Upsala brink. He bade him that could,
to make a stave in praise of that victory. Then Thorvald Hialtison, a man of Iceland of great and noble
kin that was then of the King's bodyguard, sang this
stave:

Fare to Fyrisfield, ye wolf-folk, as many as be an-hunger'd!
Night-Riders' stallions, bait at the western garth!
There be the black gems of corpse-dew: true 'tis, 'neath
    the spear-din,
Meat enough for the wolves' feast Eric hath cut down there.

The King gave Thorvald a ring of half a mark of gold for every verse. Men say that Thorvald made no other verses save these either before or since.

It was dark night when King Eric came home. The Queen met him in the door. Very big he seemed in his battered war-gear and his great horned helm. He walked somewhat heavily, but he carried his head high and kingly. And now, as he stepped into the bright light of the doorway, the Queen suddenly had sight of his face, and, with that, the question she was ready to ask him froze in her throat. Seeing her there to meet him, he checked in mid-stride, then passed on his way into the hall, as if the sight of her at that time was more than he could well bear to look upon.

XVI

Valhalla

FROM beyond those lampless depths where the last dim beam of the last star is dissolved in the eternal dark, immortal eyes looked on Fyrisfield: the eyes of the great Father of All, sitting on an high seat that seemed carved out of coppery-louring thunderclouds, and inlaid with those colours which are on the sea at sundown, and beaded and gemmed with stars of the night. And the appearance of His breast and shoulders and sinewy arms and the great thighs and thews of Him, that were partly shown and partly veiled, was as the appearance of the vast-rearing walls and headlong naked slopes of bare rock mountains, when the grey that goes before the dawn first stirs in those unwinged heights of air, and the coverlets of cloud roll back, and darkness creeps like a garment down, and the cold and prodigious limbs seem to awake out of slumber, and from the remoteness of small and narrow valleys, deep down where men have their little dwellings, a cock crows for the day. Surely to look upon the face of him, which was ruddy like a sea-cliff of red earth where a low-wheeling sun shines fair upon it, seen against the azure of a summer sea, was to find answers to many riddles and the comfort of many fears and sorrows.

At His either shoulder those ravens of his, like two black clouds, shadowed with their wings. There was darkness about the high seat and a music passing all music imagined by the mind of man, speaking those things which no tongue can utter, but men's hearts know them. And there were shapes about the high seat and above it, titanic, unclear, without stability, mountains, and giant forms of living creatures, and sleet and snows, and bearded stars travelling, and cities depopulate, and wild seas, and dreadful wolds, and forests, and burnings, and shapes and semblances of the enormous dead: all these blown by in a mist on a mighty wind that blew round about Him. And that is the wind of Eternity; and save the All-Father there is none can abide the cold of that wind nor sit in that seat: not even a God, not even those gray-faced Maidens who carve and spin beside the Well which is beneath the tree Yggdrasill; nor endure to comprehend at once all things, past, present, and to come, as, sitting there, the All-Father comprehendeth them.

Now thronged the Einheriar into Valhalla, smoking from the fight, innumerable as the multitudinous clouds in a mackerel sky at eve, heroes of bliss, of many lands, chosen from many generations of men; and the voice of their talk and deep-echoing laughter was like the sounding of the sea, and they were like unto Gods in stature and seeming, and their weapons and rich apparel like to a sunset glory in a summer garden after rain.

On a sudden our Father Odin lifted up a hand, and there was darkness in heaven all save the light of the Father's face, and all they stood up and waited in the listening gloom. And now was a noise far off, like lashing rain among leaves in a forest, and with it a rolling as of thunders far away, and pale lightnings flickered afar and vanished and flickered again through the night. Very slowly at first, then with swift strides, it drew nearer, until the roar of the tempest was like the roar of cataracts fed to fury by a cloud-burst among mountains. Then lightnings streamed in rivers of molten steel and silver from the roof-beams of that hall, which is lofty as the tent of night, and the Einheriar clashed their weapons together and shouted with a shout that was heard above the deafening thunder: "Hail to the choosers! the storm raisers! Hail to the shield-mays of the Lord of Spears, the Father of Ages, the Loving One! Hail to the lords of earth whom they bring to join our fellowship!"

Therewith, their flying steeds swooping and balancing on the gale like sea-gulls in wild weather, their spear-heads and helms of gold a-sparkle in the lightning-flare, those Maidens of Victory rode up the night into Valhalla. When their horses tossed their manes, rain streamed from them, and from the froth of their bitted mouths snow came, and hail and sleet from their nostrils. Terrible and beautiful to look upon were those riding Maidens, as fire or the ruinous thunderbolt. And each bare athwart her saddle-bow the bloody corpse of a dead man slain.

Nine times rode they on the whirlwind and the rain high in air above the tables of the blest in Valhalla; then

descending did obeisance unto the Most High, praising
Him and calling Him by His holy names: Thunderer,
Father of the Slain, Feared One, God of the Ravens,
Blinder of Hosts, the True One, the Almighty God.
Then each in turn showed her chosen one to the All-
Father, and craved leave to deliver him to those whose
craft it is to mend that which is broken, and put out
the arrow, and close up the wound, and wake the great
soul to receive again its proper body, now for ever fair,
for ever desirable and strong, capable of all feats and
of every pleasure that belongeth to the body of man;
but of pain or decay or dissolution as little capable as if
a man should go about to blow out the noon-day sun like
a candle, or to batter down mountain peaks by smiting
of them with a straw.

Last of all, rode forth before the All-Father's face
the Valkyrie Skogul. Like the brandishing of swords
the lightnings played about her, and her black plunging
horse champed flame. Yet sweet showed, even beneath
the byrny, the tender division of her breasts; and her
countenance was like the golden morning kissing awake
the high snow summits in the spring of the year. She
cried aloud unto Odin and said, "O God of Hosts,
Whisperer in the Wind, the Much-Knowing, I have
done Your command. Yet with some sickness of heart
I did it, thinking this should add but one jewel to Your
crown, O Our Father; but earth goeth destitute for
the need of such, and findeth not often one such in a
generation of men. Also, he died young."

But the All-Father, sitting in that seat where that wind blows which telleth of many hidden matters, bent for a while in silence His eternal eyes on that which His shield-may cherished against her bosom. Then He spake, and the sound of His voice was like the music of the evening star when deer trip lightly down the heather-sweet slopes at twilight, and the dews begin to fall. "Frontward are his wounds, and death availed but to tighten his grip on the sword-hilt. Be still and question not: I chose him first I loved the best."

·UNABRIDGED CLOSING NOTE·

[The following is a new version of the ending Note to *Styrbiorn the Strong*, which appears in the original Jonathan Cape edition. This unabridged version is supplemented with material from a draft of the Note included in Eddison's papers archived in the Leeds Public Library. Comparing Eddison's prepared draft with the published version allows the surmise that Cape may have asked Eddison to shorten and summarize his draft so that the published Note could be contained within a single page of text. Below, the text of the Cape edition's version of the Note is in italics. —P. E. Thomas]

Styrbiorn fell in 983. In England at that time Ethelred the Unready was King, and the last of the Carolingians in France. Otto II sat on the throne of the Caesars. John Zimisces was Emperor in Byzantium, or (as they called it in the North) King of the Greeks in Micklegarth. Iceland, that new republic of aristocrats founded from Norway by men who could not abide to be under the strong hand of King Harald Hairfair, had just passed her centenary. The great Earl Hakon, called by some the Mighty but by some the Ill, ruled like a King in Norway. Only in Denmark, under Harald Gormson, had Christianity as yet any sure foothold in the North.

Except a few very minor characters, all the persons mentioned in this story are historical, or at least of ancient tradition.

So too are the main facts, which may be found by the curious or the learned in the brief record entitled Þáttr Styrbjarnar Svíakappa, *printed in the* Lives of the Kings *(Formannasögur, Vol. V, pp. 245–51: Copenhagen, 1830). One reservation must be made from this statement: Styrbiorn's relations with Sigrid the Haughty have no historical basis save that they were suggested by what is known of the later career of that fatal Queen.* In the days of her widowhood, after Eric's death, she had her childhood's playmate King Harald the Grenlander and another king burnt in their beds, saying she "would weary these small kings of coming from other lands to woo her"; and, in her breach with Styrbiorn in Chapter X I have had in mind her dealings, seventeen years later, with King Olaf Tryggvason. When that admired young Bayard of the North and patron saint of muscular Christianity was imposing by logic of sword and fire the blessings of his church on Norway, he became betrothed to Queen Sigrid. Displeased, however, at her coldness toward his missionary efforts, he imprudently struck her across the mouth with his glove, saying at the same time, "What have I to do with thee, a heathen bitch?" "These words," she replied, "may likely prove thy death." No windy menace: for her hand seems to have been in it when he fell in the great sea-fight at Svoldr under a combined attack by his enemies, and not least among them King Svein Twibeard, King of Denmark, and later conqueror of England, whom Sigrid had by that time wedded as her second husband. For the rest, Sigrid's marriage to Eric and the homage paid to their son Olaf the Lap-King in his father's lifetime are matters of history.

For the description of Jomsburg and the provisions of the "Lay of the Jomsburgers" in Chapter IV, I have followed closely the account given in the *Jomsvikinga Saga* (*Flatyjarbok*, Vol. 1, p. 166, Christiania: 1860).

The verses are translations. Those in Chapters V and IX are rendered nearly line for line and word for word, and in an alliterative measure somewhat resembling the original, out of the Elder Edda. In the renderings of these extracts from the "Voluspa" in Chapter V and of the Hell-ride of Brynhild in Chapter IX, I have aimed at the almost impossible: a literal word for word translation which shall also preserve the rhythm and alliteration of the original. Alliteration gives emphasis to the alliterated words: the translation should therefore not only alliterate, but alliterate the same words as does the original. Even with languages as closely akin as English and Old Norse, such an attempt presents appalling difficulties, and I am only too conscious of my failure. At the same time I think it is by this method only that a translator can ever hope to reproduce the peculiar wild and stormy sublimity of the Eddic Poems. Sigrid's little song in Chapter III and the lament of the Jutes in Chapter XIII are also close translations: the original of the latter is given in the *Þáttr Styrbjarnar*, cited above. For my text I have in all cases followed York Powell and Vigfússon's *Corpus Poeticum Boreale*, Clarendon Press, 1883.

One thing I would add. The great classic literature of the North is, even in these days, little known save to specialists. To the plain reader (and it is him, and not learned persons, that I care about) the word "saga" has depressing associations: a complex of Wagnerian opera, Medieval German romance, antiquated poetry and mythology, and unending blood. There exists, it is true, a mass of late romantic "saga" literature, corrupted by foreign influences, and produced in an age when inspiration was fallen impotent, senile, or dead. But to class this poor bombastic fairy-story stuff with the Icelandic sagas proper is as bad as to confound Pheidias with the Graeco-Roman decadence, or (dare I say it?) Homer with Virgil.

The spirit of the North, to the inheritance of which I believe (*pace* Mr. Hilaire Belloc) our own country largely owes her greatness, is embodied in its purest form in its prose epic, the Icelandic Sagas of the classical age, such as (to name a few) *Njal's Saga*, the *Laxdale Saga*, the *Saga of Egil Skallagrimsson*, *Gisli's Saga*, and the *Saga of Hrafnkel the Priest of Frey*. There is no "Keltic Twilight" here, no barbaric exaggerations, no embroidery, no weaving of words or fancies, no boggling at truth: there is much shrewd insight into character and the springs of action, a power of direct and vivid narrative rarely matched in any other literature, much deep-seated humour and philosophy of hard and manly life. But this is not the place to do more than hint at some obvious qualities of that genius which has shed about the lives of a few great families, dwelling in lonely homesteads in distant Iceland, an atmosphere of tragic and epic grandeur like the grandeur that is about windy Ilios; bringing us, in the end, as Homer brings us, not to take sides with Greeks or Trojans, with Njal's sons or the Burners, but to ponder (somewhat perhaps as the

260

Gods may ponder) on the greatness and the pitifulness of human things.

My story is not an imitation of a Saga. I have told it in my own way. Imitations are dead lumber: but having been a reader of Sagas these twenty-five years, and having chosen such a theme and staged it in such an age, I should be foolish to deny that while the defects of this book may be mine, its merits, if it has any, must be fastened on that spirit which lives in the Sagas. Anyone, therefore, who likes this tale, can turn hopefully from it to Dasent's translation of *The Story of Burnt Njal*, or to the fine translations of *Eyrbyggja*, *Heimskringla*, etc., in William Morris's and Eirikr Magnússon's *Saga Library*.

E. R. Eddison

THE WRITING OF *Styrbiorn the Strong*

Paul Edmund Thomas

IN his previously unpublished Letter of Introduction
to his younger brother Colin, Eddison declares that
"Styrbiorn's name has sounded in my memory like a drum
ever since, twenty years ago, I first read the passing reference to him in the *Eyrbyggja Saga*." That reading may have
occurred before he turned eighteen: it was in May 1900 that
Eddison obtained the Morris & Magnússon translation of
Eyrbyggja Saga, entitled *The Story of the Ere-Dwellers*, published as volume 2 of the exquisitely bound Saga Library.
At forty, Eddison saw his first and most famous work,
The Worm Ouroboros, come so gorgeously off the press at
Jonathan Cape in the spring of 1922, and he decided it was
time to follow the drumbeats to their source.

In May 1922, the novelist H. Rider Haggard sent two
letters to Eddison in praise of *The Worm Ouroboros*, saying,
in the first, "Since Morris died there has been too little pure
Romance, and surely never was Romance more needed in
the world," and in the second, "If you write another of the
sort, shorten, simplify, and have one predominant male
and ditto female character, and one supreme love interest: something in the line of *Eric Brighteyes* if I may quote
works of my own." If Eddison read Haggard's historical

novel of the Viking age, he made no written comment on it that survives, but his extant notes from those days reveal that by the summer of 1922 Eddison was planning a new work that developed generally in accord with Haggard's advice, which is not to say that Eddison necessarily took Haggard's advice.

One of Eddison's earliest notes for *Styrbiorn*, jotted on July 30, 1922, raises more questions than it answers about what he may have been reading and thinking that summer as he prepared to write:

> Grand instance of right and wrong method of telling history: "In this there were *temples of idols*, or as the pagans said, *many and powerful deities*." This is the whole philosophy in a nutshell.

Whether Eddison was quoting directly or translating from a text is unknown, but the last sentence allows the surmise that Eddison might have written the note amid reflections on the nature of historical novels and about the specific approach he wanted to adopt toward his historical material: to take the material on its own terms, in its tenth-century Scandinavian context, and to view it, as far as possible, without imposing modern evaluative judgments on it. The letter to Colin, in which Eddison explains his approach, supports this assertion because it reads as if the novel has already been finished, when in fact the letter was the first piece that Eddison wrote for *Styrbiorn*. He finished the letter to Colin by August 6, 1922, and dispatched

it to his typist, Edith Brinton, along with another letter
that told her, "I am starting on a new book: a historical
story this time about people who really lived in this world,
in the Viking age in Sweden a thousand years ago, the age
of the great classic saga literature of the north, which I
have studied these twenty years and which I love more
than any other."

By August 22, Eddison had finished the first chapter,
"On King Olaf's Howe," and sent that off to Brinton as
well. He completed no more chapters before the end of
the year, but he likely began reading extensively in the
specific period history. Just at this time, August 1922,
Eddison obtained John Sephton's translation of *The Saga
of King Olaf Tryggvason*, which he may have read chiefly
for information about Queen Sigrid. Also at this time, and
during the next three years, Eddison devoted considerable
energy to reading the two massive volumes entitled *The
Viking Age: The Early History, Manners, and Customs of the
Ancestors of the English-Speaking Nations*, by Paul Belloni
Du Chaillu. In addition, Eddison's notes show that he was
reading about the landscapes and the flora and fauna of
Sweden in Joseph Acerbi's *Travels through Sweden, Finland,
and Lapland, to the North Cape, in the Years 1798 and 1799*.

After Christmas in 1922, Eddison went on a holiday
with his family to Sidmouth on the coast of Devonshire
("lovely Devon, where it rains eight days out of seven").
There, on the last day of the year, Eddison began the
second chapter, "Thorgnyr the Lawman." On January 5,
1923, he may have taken a night walk on the seaboard

of Sidmouth and watched the winter waves pound the Jurassic cliffs below Salcombe Hill because the image struck him enough to note it down on his return to the hotel:

> Sea at night, moonless, breaking on a beach.
> Behind first row of breakers, others (3 or 4
> at a time sometimes) come bodying out of
> the darkness, like white ghostships rushing
> broadside on the flood. The effect of terrific
> speed is made by the fact that the foaming crest
> (the only part seen under these conditions, as
> the night is black) begins on a short strip of
> wave and spreads rapidly right & left. Use this
> ominously and terribly: perhaps Eric, having
> staked the approaches to Sigtun, stands by the
> firth in the dark and sees it, and thinks it points
> at Styrbiorn rushing on his destruction.

Eddison used the noted image just as he first thought he might, for it appears in the penultimate paragraph of Chapter XIV, "King Eric's Hosting." This winter Channel surf also seems to have inspired the elegiac "Jomsburg Sea-Walls," which became the eleventh chapter, and which opens to show us a chastened and newly banished Styrbiorn staring at "rolling surges sweeping and pausing and falling and rising again" and listening to "the swelling roar of the breaker as it rode on, the thud and thunder of its fall, and the grinding hiss of the shingle in the backwash, as if wrath, which is older than the world and older than the Gods, drew in its breath once again, pondering some greater mischief." Before the week of that vacation was up, Eddison completed "Jomsburg Sea-Walls" and also the piece that became the novel's sublime final chapter, "Valhalla." He then returned to London, finished Chapter II, and sent all three chapters to Brinton on January 23.

In working almost simultaneously on three unconnected chapters from the beginning, middle, and end of his story, Eddison displays a characteristic composing method: after much contemplation and making extensive outlines and plot summaries, Eddison would reach a point of thoughtful certainty with his stories that allowed him to work on whatever section his muse was at that moment hovering over, ready to guide, with rapid wingbeats, his pen across the page. Eddison's last, unfinished novel, *The Mezentian Gate*, for which he similarly wrote the beginning and ending chapters before working on the middle, best exemplifies his method of exhaustive planning prior to composing whatever chapter seemed readiest in his imagination, like a chef having several sauté pans on the fire at once and giving each a flick of the wrist as needed.

Eddison began the third chapter, "Queen Sigrid the Haughty," on January 27, 1923, but then his progress appears to have ceased for nearly sixteen months. However, February 1923 found him writing to Bertha Phillpotts, the noted scholar of Old Norse literature and Mistress of Girton College, Cambridge: "I am anxious to get some information about Jomsburg . . . I do not even know whether the site of the burg is known." Given the tone of this letter, it is probable that Eddison continued to research and read history extensively throughout 1923.

Eddison returned to his writing desk in May 1924 and finished the fourth chapter, "Jomsburg," between May 3 and June 8. He also resumed "Queen Sigrid the Haughty," the third chapter, which had lain unfinished for more than a year, and completed it by June 14. Tracking his progress over the subsequent four months is speculative, but it is probable that he was working on the sixth chapter, "The Dane-King's Daughter," and the eighth chapter, "The King and the Queen," in the second half of 1924.

In mid-August Eddison received a letter from the famous Irish novelist and poet James Stephens, author of *The Crock of Gold*, who praised *The Worm Ouroboros* and went on to say, "The real thing that I should like to know is, that you are working; and, having given your astonishing talent such a header into such a sea, that you will not delay too long in advertising it again." Eddison responded on September 11 by explaining that his daily work with the Board of Trade, where, at that time, he was the comptroller of the Companies Department, kept him from spending more time at his writing desk:

> I am writing another—of a different kind and
> half the length. But as my normal days from
> 10:00 till 7:00 are spent on the prosaic business
> of Departmental administration (which, and
> not, alas, Worms and their tails, procures my
> livelihood), I'm afraid it will be some time
> before this new offspring sees the light.

Eddison's professional career at the Board of Trade did not go unrecognized, and the end of 1924 found him gratefully standing among those receiving the distinction of appointment as a Companion of the Most Distinguished Order of Saint Michael and Saint George by King George V. He also managed to finish the piece that became the novel's fifth chapter, "Yule in Denmark," five days before Christmas.

Eddison may have begun 1925 with renewed determination to finish the novel in that calendar year. In the first week of January he began what became the ninth chapter, "A Banquet in Upsala." Before completing it, he started the subsequent and pivotal tenth chapter, "Broken Meats in Upsala," on April 25 and finished both chapters on July 8, 1925. He then worked steadily through the rest of the year. He wrote chapters XII and XIII, "The Cowing of the Dane-King" and "The Sailing of the Fleet" between the last week of August and mid-October. He started right in on the swelling and climactic fourteenth and fifteenth chapters, "King Eric's Hosting" and "Fyrisfield," and completed them on November 28, 1925, just four days after his forty-third birthday.

The book was then mostly complete, though he did some revising in December. Nevertheless, Eddison did not send it out for consideration until a couple of months later, probably because he wanted to give the work a short test of time to make sure, upon rereading in subsequent weeks, that it continued to satisfy him. When he did send it out, he experienced none of the whips and scorns of time and none of the spurns that patient writers (grunt-ing and sweating under their weary lives) must take from the unworthy in our day. There were no cold rebuffs from smug and jaded agents, no lengthy silences from swamped and indifferent publishers in those fair days of 1926: Eddison sent the manuscript directly to Jonathan Cape in February; Cape did not hand it to a reader but instead personally read it in the first week of March, even though he must have been preoccupied with his house's imminent publication of the first public edition of T. E. Lawrence's *Seven Pillars of Wisdom;* Cape offered terms for publish-ing *Styrbiorn* on March 11, 1926; a draft contract followed three days later, which was amended and signed before the end of the month. A done deal, and all in less than six weeks.

On May 13, 1926, Cape asked Eddison for a hundred-word interest-grabbing description of *Styrbiorn* to go out in Cape's advance catalog. Eddison returned the follow-ing the next day:

> The Swedish Prince called Styrbiorn the
> Strong, after a meteoric career in which he
> shook the lands of the Baltic, fell in the year
> 983, still in his early youth, in the attempt to
> wrest the kingdom from his uncle. The writer
> follows history closely. His intimate knowledge
> of the Viking civilization and spirit is taken at
> first hand from the ancient literature of the
> North. In his swift dramatic narrative he takes
> no sides, but leaves his actors—Styrbiorn, King

Eric the Victorious, and his fatal Queen—to
impress their personalities on the reader by
their own words and actions.

Given a hundred-word limit, Eddison does not discuss
the sagas, but his description of his novel as a "swift dramatic narrative" in which "he takes no sides," highlights
the saga influence. Eddison's admiration for the nonpar-
tisan, nonjudgmental narrative voices of the best of the
Old Norse sagas cannot be overemphasized. He loved the
saga writers' technique of relating actions baldly, without commentary, without didacticism, without an overt
attempt to shape readers' interpretations or predispose
their opinions, regardless of the nature of the actions.
Thus shocking scenes, like the slaying of lovely Swanhild
in the *Volsunga Saga*, are related merely factually, without
explanation, and without any condemnation of the Iago-
like counselor Bikki, who contrives her brutal death, or of
the Goth King Jormunrek, who orders it, and so the stark
horror and monstrous injustice of the moment howl at
us from the silence between the sentences. And thus the
title character in *Egil's Saga* can rise at dawn, gouge out a
man's eye with his finger, and then, before breakfast has
ended, burn a whale bone and carve runes that help heal a
sick young woman, all without any moral comment from
the narrator or introspection from Egil, which leaves us
wondering whether Egil perceives the irony in his para-
doxical behavior and whether the terse narrator wanted
to leave us wondering just that. The plain and unanalytic
manner in which saga narrators relate action frequently

makes a saga seem less like a novel and more like a drama, and it is not by accident that Eddison calls his narrative "dramatic" and his three main characters "actors" who "impress their personalities on the reader," not filtered through the discretionary judgments of a partisan narra-tor but "by their own words and actions."

By not taking sides among his principals, Eddison knew he was launching his readers onto a morally turbulent sea. When, in Chapter IX, Styrbiorn hears the tale of Gudrun and Sigurd, Styrbiorn's thoughts on that tragic story could aptly describe his own life, had he known the ending, and thus aptly describe Eddison's novel, too: "It was a strange unlucky tale, and not easy for a man to see the rights and wrongs of it." Eddison knew he was risking putting off some readers who might prefer fiction with more moral clarity, more agreeable characters, and perhaps a more amiable ending.

But Eddison probably did not mind losing readers with such preferences. In *Styrbiorn* he aspired to no conventions of popular romance; rather, he aspired to achieve what he found in the sagas: tragedy, and a grandeur worthy of tragedy. As he says in his Unabridged Closing Note, in the best of the sagas there exists "an atmosphere of tragic and epic grandeur like the grandeur that is about windy Ilios; bringing us, in the end, as Homer brings us, not to take sides with Greeks or Trojans, with Njal's sons or the Burners, but to ponder (somewhat perhaps as the Gods may ponder) on the greatness and the pitifulness of human things." Eddison's extant notes show that he planned the "architecture" of his story to be structured like a classical tragedy, with Sigrid cast, like Patroklos in the *Iliad*, as the force of fate that sets the tragic figures in violent conflict with each other and the tragic end in motion. The "Sigrid entanglement," Eddison notes, "is like Desdemona's handkerchief: without it all might have gone well." As a force of fate, Eddison compares Sigrid to a "match to the vetch-stack," who, having "lighted the fire, is swept away in the blaze." For King Eric and Styrbiorn, who just one day earlier "were ever in company and were so glad of each other that it was a wonder to see" (Chapter VIII), the Sigrid entanglement breaks all bonds of love and drives them to their tragic finish at Fyrisfield. Eddison describes the ashen-hearted Eric after Fyrisfield in a sublime note written sometime before the summer of 1924: "Eric, in the desert of his victory and cold loftiness of duty done, alone, estranged from his wife, bereft of the young man in whom his hopes were placed, stands like a lonely sorrowful mountain peak in the kinless twilight." Eddison concludes by emphasizing the hollowness and the tragic irony of Eric's post-Fyrisfield title: "King Eric the Victorious."

In September 1926, *Styrbiorn the Strong* was published in the United Kingdom by Jonathan Cape and in the United States by Albert & Charles Boni. One of the early admirers of the novel was Eddison's oldest friend, Arthur Ransome, beloved author of *Swallows and Amazons* and many other books, who praised both *The Worm Ouroboros* and *Styrbiorn* in the October 1926 issue of Jonathan Cape's

Now & Then periodical. There may be no better voice than Ransome's, a voice of lifelong friendship for Eddison, to close this Afterword:

> In *Styrbiorn the Strong* he is following to
> its source one of the main streams of his
> inspiration . . . This new book of Eddison's,
> wholly different in conception [from *The Worm
> Ouroboros*] but with the same Scandinavian
> roots, will weave a similar spell over those
> whose hearts are in the north, as his is.

Minneapolis
October 2011

E. R. (Eric Rücker) Eddison (1882–1945) so loved the William Morris and George Webbe Dasent translations of Old Norse sagas that, as a teenager in northern England, he taught himself to read Old Icelandic. He studied classics at Trinity College, Oxford; entered civil service with the Board of Trade; translated *Egil's Saga;* and wrote five novels, including the fantasy classic *The Worm Ouroboros.* His foundational works of fantasy were highly praised by J. R. R. Tolkien, C. S. Lewis, H. P. Lovecraft, and Ursula K. Le Guin.

Paul Edmund Thomas is a literary scholar of E. R. Eddison and J. R. R. Tolkien. He annotated and introduced the Dell editions of *The Worm Ouroboros* and *Zimiamvia: A Trilogy* (which contains, in one volume, Eddison's *Mistress of Mistresses, A Fish Dinner in Memison,* and the unfinished *The Mezentian Gate,* as well as previously unpublished writings). He is an intellectual property attorney with Fredrikson & Byron, P.A., in Minneapolis, Minnesota.